Alan Garner OBE is a novelist and folklorist who first rose to prominence in the 1960s with his seminal fantasies *The Weirdstone of Brisingamen* and *The Moon of Gomrath*, both rooted in the mythology and landscape of his native Cheshire. This long-awaited novel completes the *Weirdstone* trilogy.

In the intervening years Alan has written many other award-winning and critically acclaimed novels, including *The Owl Service* (winner of the Guardian Award and the Carnegie Medal), *Elidor* and *Red Shift*. While these earlier novels were published for children, his later books, such as *The Stone Book Quartet*, *Strandloper* and *Thursbitch*, have been intended for adults and have sealed his reputation as one of the country's very greatest writers.

Boneland unites these two strands of work: it is a novel for adults, concluding a trilogy that was begun for children. A stunning novel of poetry, landscape, history and the enduring resonance of myth, it will be read and di~~scussed~~ for years to come.

From the reviews of *Bonela~~nd~~*

'Alan Garner's novel *Bonel~~and~~* ...... at makes Garner such a uniqu~~e genius~~ ...... se, spare vividness, terrifying psychological subtlety and the kind of visual imagination that makes everything, from stones to stars, strange.'

Rowan Williams, *New Statesman*, Books of the Year

'Lovers of *The Weirdstone of Brisingamen* and *The Moon of Gomrath* should try this opaque resolution of the trilogy.'

Financial Times, Books of the Year

'Sequels and prequels were everywhere . . . Alan Garner – a mere 50 years on – concluding his classic sequence of children's novels with the adult volume *Boneland*.'

Justine Jordan, *Guardian*, Books of the Year

'Reads as if Garner has hewn each word from rock and spent decades diamond-cutting every line . . . Intense, obsessive, and dreamlike . . . one of the strangest and most beautiful books I've ever read.'   Julie Bertagna, *Scotsman*, Books of the Year

'*Boneland* has all the simplicity and strength of the best of Garner. The story is thrilling, both in itself and as a resolution of the stories begun in *The Weirdstone of Brisingamen* and *The Moon of Gomrath*. Those who were young when the first two books came out (as I was) won't be disappointed: this was worth waiting for.'   Philip Pullman

'He deploys short, accurate words better than anyone else writing in English today, and he makes it look simple. *Boneland* is the strangest, but also the strongest of Garner's books. It feels like a capstone to a career that has taken him, as a writer, to remarkable places, and returned him to the same place he started, to the landscape of Alderley Edge and to the sleepers under the hill.'   Neil Gaiman, *The Times*

'From Harry Potter to *The Hunger Games*, adults have been enthusiastically reading children's books over recent years. Garner predates the crossover phenomenon by decades, but he has never been just a children's writer: he's far richer, odder and deeper than that.'   *Guardian*

ALAN GARNER

Boneland

FOURTH ESTATE • *London*

Fourth Estate
An imprint of HarperCollins*Publishers*
77–85 Fulham Palace Road
Hammersmith
London W6 8JB

This Fourth Estate paperback edition published 2013
1

First published in Great Britain by Fourth Estate in 2012

Copyright © Alan Garner 2012

Alan Garner asserts the moral right to be identified as the author of this work

A catalogue record for this book is available from the British Library

ISBN 978-0-00-746325-1

Set in Minion by
Palimpsest Book Production Limited, Falkirk, Stirlingshire

Printed and bound in Great Britain by Clays Ltd, St Ives plc

MIX
Paper from
responsible sources
FSC
www.fsc.org
FSC™ C007454

FSC™ is a non-profit international organisation established to promote
the responsible management of the world's forests. Products carrying the
FSC label are independently certified to assure consumers that they come
from forests that are managed to meet the social, economic and
ecological needs of present and future generations,
and other controlled sources.

Find out more about HarperCollins and the environment at
www.harpercollins.co.uk/green

For the worth of two Marks and a Bob

The dream was wonder, but the terror was great. We must keep the dream, whatever the terror.

The Epic of Gilgamesh, Tablet VII, line 75

The stones have no rosetta.

Mark Edmonds, *Prehistory in the Peak*, p.96

Hit hade a hole on þe ende and on ayþer syde,
And ouergrowen with gresse in glodes aywhere,
And al watz holȝ inwith, nobot an olde caue,
Or a creuisse of an olde cragge . . .

It had a hole on the end and on either side,
And overgrown with grass in clumps everywhere,
And all was hollow within, nothing but an old cave,
Or a crevice of an old crag . . .

Sir Gawain and the Green Knight, lines 2180–4

'Listen. I'll tell you. I've got to tell you.'
'A scratch, Colin.'
'I must tell you.'
'Just a scratch.'
'I will.'
'There.'
'I shall.'
'Done.'

He cut the veil of the rock; the hooves clattered the bellowing waters below him in the dark. The lamp brought the moon from the blade, and the blade the bull from the rock. The ice rang.

He took life in his mouth, spat red over hand on the cave wall. The bull roared. Around, above him, the trample of the beasts answered; the stags, the hinds, the horses, the bulls, and the trace of old dreams. The ice rang. He held the lamp and climbed among antlers necks ears eyes horns haunches, the limbs, the nostrils, the rutting, the dancers; from the cave to the crack. He pushed the lamp at the dark and followed his shoulder, his head twisted, through the hill along the seam of grit, by the nooks of the dead. He slipped out; pinched the lamp, and crawled between slabs into the gash of Ludcruck on snow.

The colours and webs faded and he saw the world. The ice had dropped from the two cliffs flat in the gap. He braced himself against each side of stone, and moved over the fall.

He found them lying together. He tried to touch her and the child through the ice. He saw his echo, but they had no echo. Though the eyes met, they did not speak. They were not him. Where the crag had shed, spirit faces looked down from the scar, rough, knuckled, green; and grass hung over the ledges.

He passed where the cleft opened more than a spear length. The sky was blue, icicles shone; the sun played, but could not reach the floor. He went along, up, around, and left Ludcruck hole by the arch to the hill.

He met the footsteps, woman and child, and walked against them, back above the river, cobbles banging in the melt of summer flood, until a fold of land shut off the sound and he came to the lodge. He opened the hide and went in.

He lay for one day. He lay for two days. He lay for three days.

'Colin. Colin?'

A face was leaning over him, concentrated, checking. He heard and saw, but did not wake.

Next, he was in the ward, and a panel in the ceiling rattled.

'Cup of tea, diddums?'

'No. Thanks.'

'Coffee, my love?'

'No. Thanks.'

'Water, pet?'

'Please. Yes.'

'Chin up, chicken.'

A hand lifted his head, and another put the hard glass between his teeth.

'Thanks.'

Someone wiped his beard. The colours and webs faded. He saw the world.

'Hello, Colin.' A doctor looked down at him.

'Hello.'

'Well, all seems to be fine. You can go home tomorrow.'

'Why not now? Now. Please. That was the agreement.'

'I don't advise it.' The doctor went to the desk and spoke to the sister. Colin worked a finger under the plastic strip around his wrist that showed his name and number and date of birth and tugged to snap it. It did not move. He tried to force it over his hand. The plastic bit into the skin. He managed to get another finger through and lodged the plastic in the crease of each first joint, and pulled again. The white band did not slacken. He blocked his mind against it, shut his eyes and willed the hands apart. He held the pain as ecstasy. It could not feel, and he would not give. He would not give. It could not feel. He would not give. He would not. The band broke, and he fell back, triumphant.

'There we are, cherub.'

He opened his eyes. A nurse had snipped the band with scissors.

He reached behind the locker for his backpack, took off the gown and dragged on his clothes; no more a thing.

'You're discharging yourself, Colin. I'd be happier if you stayed until after breakfast tomorrow. You do understand?'

'I understand, sister. But I'd like to have a taxi, please.'

'It's in your interest to stay.'

'I know it is. But I want to go. I want to go home. I need to. I want to go now.'

'Avoid alcohol until you've seen your own doctor. Remember.'

'I'll remember.'

A porter wheeled him to the main hall. With each passage from the ward to the air he felt himself return. The taxi was waiting.

'Where are we for, squire?' said the driver.

'Church Quarry, please.'

'Where's that?'

'I'll show you.'

'Best sit at the front, then.'

Colin got in and held the backpack on his knee.

'Done your seat belt?'

'Sorry.'

The driver reached over and ran the belt across Colin's chest between his arms and the backpack and locked it. They drove round the car park to the road.

'Which way?' said the driver.

Colin's cheek was on the backpack.

'Don't nod off, mate, else we'll never get home.'

'Sorry. Go by Trugs.'

'Got you.'

They left the town into the falling sun, away from the straight walls, the corridors without shadow, the flatnesses, along roads and lanes that bent, dipped and lifted, copying the land. Colin's head drooped.

'What line of business are you in, then?' said the driver.

'Sorry?'

'What's your job?'

'Ah. Survey. M45. At the moment.'

'It wants widening.'

'I'm measuring it.'

'Comes in handy sometimes.'

'Yes?'

'M6, M42, M45, M1.'

'How do you mean?'

'It misses the worst of the traffic.'

'May I have a little air?'

'Sure. So what's this survey you're doing?'

'Plotting dwarfs.'

The driver looked at him.

'Only the anomalous. Bear right at The Black Greyhound,' said Colin.

'Bloody Norah.'

'The main work is MERLIN.'

'What's that?'

'Acronym.'

'Oh. To keep them bridges up.'

'Turn right here,' said Colin. The taxi wove between potholes along a farm track beside the wood. 'At the next tree will do fine.'

'You all right, mate?'

'Perfect,' said Colin. 'Thank you very much.'

He walked into the silence of the wood and the quarry and his Bergli hut. He put the key to the door but he could not feel the lock. Sweat ran and his mouth was dry. Light shone on the log planks. He turned his head towards it in the dusk. It was a torch, dazzling him.

'You sure you're all right, mate?' said the driver.

'Perhaps a little help,' said Colin. He slid down the doorframe. 'How remiss of me.'

'Come here. Let's be having you.' The driver took the key, unlocked the door and opened it. 'Where's the switch?'

'For what?'

'The electric.'

'I don't use it.'

'By the cringe.'

The driver put his arms under Colin's shoulders and lifted him across the threshold. He swung his torch to see the room, then hefted Colin along the floor and laid him down on a bunk that was against the wall.

'The lamp's on the table,' said Colin. 'Matches in the drawer.'

The driver looked. 'And what's this effort?'

'Tilley. Loosen the pump to release any pressure.'

'What pump?'

'The knurled projection on the top of the reservoir. Give it a quarter turn to the left and retighten. Open the jar of meths

5

and dip the preheater in. When it's soaked, clip the preheater around the vaporiser stem, light it with a match and slide it up under the glass. When the meths begins to expire, give four full firm rhythmic strokes on the pump, like so: "*Here* comes a *candle* to *light* you to *bed*"; then as the flame dies, turn on the lamp and the mantle will ignite audibly and burn yellow. After thirty seconds give several strokes on the pump until the mantle is white and the lamp is making a steady hiss. What's the matter?'

The driver was laughing. 'Stone the crows! You're summat else, you are!'

'What? Where? How many?' Colin got himself to the table. He pulled a chair across, sat heavily, and lit the Tilley lamp. His hands shook but his pumping brought the hissing white.

'How many?'

'How many what?' said the driver.

'Crows.'

The driver's phone rang. 'Hi, Fay. I'm with a customer. The job from the hospital. Eh? You're breaking up.'

'A figure of speech,' said Colin. 'Of course.'

'I'll ring you back. Cheers.'

'So selfish of me to detain you,' said Colin.

'You're all right, mate. Part of the service.'

'Thank you. Thank you. That's generous. Most generous. Should I need a taxi in the future, will you be able to drive me?'

'Sure. Here's our card. Give us a bell.'

'But I'd like you to do it, personally. What's your name?'

'Call me Bert.'

'I mean your full name.'

'Bert Forster. But ask for Bert.' He wrote on the card.

'Thank you. Bert.' Colin held out his hand. 'Whisterfield. Colin Whisterfield.'

'Pleased to meet you, Colin. Now, how are we going to sort you?'

6

'I'm feeling better; much better. I'll be fine.'

'Can I get you owt?'

'No. No. I'll sit here a while and then go to bed. If you'll pass me a glass, there's a rather good malt over there. I only wish I could invite you to join me.'

The driver put the glass and the bottle on the table and Colin poured the whisky with a steady hand.

'Right then, Colin. I'll be off.'

'Yes. Thanks for all you've done, Bert. Good night. If you could close the curtains . . .'

'No problem.'

'I hadn't finished answering your question.'

'What question?'

'I was saying. Multi-element-radio-linked-interferometer-network.'

'So you were. Cheers, mate.'

Colin made a fire and sat at the table through the night until the day showed. Then he put out the lamp, sprawled on his bunk; and he slept.

He woke, drank, blew a fire heap, ate meat, and left the lodge. He took smouldering moss and the lamp and went into Ludcruck from the Bearstone so that he did not cross the icefall.

He lit the lamp and worked through the grit past the nooks of the dead. The beasts trampled, but he did not stay. He lowered himself over the lip of the cliff inside the hill and climbed in the flicker, seeing nothing outside the globe in which he hung, hearing only the waters below, down to the great cave that was night, and the Stone that was its being, though it could be held in a fist.

The Stone was the womb of things. Nothing before it was made, and with it the spirits had chopped the marrow from the rock. It lay among the glint of its making; and the shining river ran beneath.

He put the lamp aside and sat a while, moving his thought. Then he stood and he stamped and he danced on the flakes and he sang. The chinking filled the cave, answering between the walls and the sky of the roof. He turned about the black Stone. He became the sounds, and was with the voices of the old, and the voices of the old were with him.

His step pressed the flakes; and from them under him rose moonlight, which grew with the dance, until it quelled the lamp. The moon lifted into him and flowed from bone to bone; along his spine and every rib, gleamed at his fingers, filled his skull, broke through his eyes, and brought pictures to his tongue.

Wolf! Wolf! Grey Wolf! I am calling for you!

Far away the Grey Wolf heard, and came.

Here am I, the Grey Wolf.

The woman. The child.

That is not Trouble. The Trouble is yet to come. Sit up on me, the Grey Wolf.

He sat up on the shoulder. The Grey Wolf struck the damp earth and ran, higher than the trees, lower than the clouds, and each leap measured a mile; from his feet flint flew, spring spouted, lake surged and mixed with gravel dirt, and birch bent to the ground. Hare crouched, boar bristled, crow called, owl woke, and stag began to bell. And the Grey Wolf stopped.

They were at the Hill of Death and Life.

Get down from me, the Grey Wolf, and gather the red rock, the white rock, the green rock, the blue rock, the brown rock, the black rock, and bring them here.

He got down from the Grey Wolf and went about the Hill of Death and Life. He gathered the red rock, the white rock, the green rock, the blue rock, the brown rock, the black rock, and brought them to where the Grey Wolf was.

He sat up on the shoulder, and the Grey Wolf struck the damp earth and ran, higher than the trees, lower than the clouds, and each leap measured a mile; from his feet flint flew, spring spouted, lake surged and mixed with gravel dirt, and birch bent to the ground. Hare crouched, boar bristled, crow called, owl woke, and stag began to bell. The Grey Wolf came to the great cave above the waters.

Hold the Stone. Grind thunder.

No one, not the living, not the dead, has touched the Stone. It is a spirit thing.

Long hair, short wit. I, the Grey Wolf, am speaking. Do it.

He got down and held the Stone in his fist. He put the rocks in among the flakes and bore on them with the Stone's point; twisting their roughness, grating, churning. The rocks crumbled to sand beneath the weight. There was no moon but the cry of the grains of every hue, swirling, streaming about him, in him, through him, which became wind and thunder that picked him so that all that kept him was his hand on the Stone, his body tossed by the wind, until he could hold no more, and the thunder took him through the hill in a ball of rainbow and set him on the ground, by the river, under the sky.

He tasted lightning. He smelt it. The air was jags and spots. The Stone came as a cloud with flame from the Tor of Ghosts. The sky was riven in noise enough to break the hills. The land changed colours, and what was flat was black and what was steep was white; and the Stone flared and rent the slot of Ludcruck.

He dropped, his eyes shut, seeing only the wind. He sang, and with each song the earth shook. He lay, and was quiet; the earth stilled. His breath sounded in the great cave. Yet he lay a while, until the last quake died and his hands felt only the grasp of snow.

He opened his eyes. He was lying on the floor and the lamp shone. His hands bled from clutched shards. The Stone was in its place among the powdered rocks and had not moved.

Wolf. Wolf. Grey Wolf.

There was no answer.

He cupped the lamp in his palm and climbed, not feeling the pain as he pulled on the cliff.

Ludcruck was filled with summer. The ice had gone and the green mist of growing lit the spirit faces that looked out from the walls among fern, grass and holly along the twisting length.

The woman and the child lay in beds of eight-petalled white avens flower. He touched their faces and held their hands. The bodies were soft. He carried them out of Ludcruck to the hill. Here was snow and knars of grit stood draped.

He went to where a stack rose on ground above the valley and laid the bodies down. He snapped the icicles, clearing the way. He took the woman and climbed, and rested her on the snow at the stack top and opened her clothing.

She was lovely. Her cheeks were sunken, but had been so before when meat was late. Her nose was pinched, but he had seen that in winter. Only the hollow middle of her eye, the jaw and the stain on her shoulders her buttocks and behind her legs said that she would not come back. He loosed her hair, and laid it to either side of the sweet face.

Then he brought the child, wrapped in hare skin, and unbound it.

He left them together on the stack, where no beast would reach and steal, but birds could take them to the circle of life in air and earth, and he turned to the lodge. At the end of day, he looked out and saw that they were safe under ravens.

'Risselty-rosselty, hey pomposity,

Knickerty-knackerty

Now, now, now.'

Colin took his bicycle and pedalled along the track to the road, adjusted his helmet, and crossed into Artists Lane. He stopped, lifted his feet and let the gradient take him down the dip slope of the Edge.

'Risselty-rosselty, hey donny-dossity,

Knickerty-knackerty, rustical quality,
Willow tree wallowty
Now, now, now.'
He swept round the blind corner at Brynlow, past The Topps
and The Butts to the Cross.
'Risselty-rosselty, hey bombossity,
Knickerty-knackerty, rustical quality,
Willow tree wallowty, hey donny-dossity,
Risselty-rosselty
Now, now, now.'
He reached the main road and without looking right or left
or touching the brakes went straight over from Artists Lane to
Welsh Row. He coasted past Nut Tree and New House as far
as Gatley Green until he came to the bypass and the railway
bridge and had to pedal, after two point seven eight four three
kilometres of free energy; approximately. Then it was Soss Moss,
Chelford and Dingle Bank, to the telescope.
He punched the door code and went into the control room.
'Afternoon, Owen.'
'Hi, Colin.' The duty controller turned in his chair away from
the encompassing desk, the monitors and computers and the
clocks of other time. 'What are you doing?'
'I want to check the data.'
'You're a liability. You know that?'
'Have you got the printouts?'
'And R.T.'s after your head.'
'Wellaway.'
'He's found you're spending time on M45. Says you're wasting
the budget.'
'Am I, now?'
'Don't push it. He thinks you're not here.'
'I can change that.'
'Colin. You're off sick.'
'So I don't feel sick.'

11

'Listen. We worry about you. You're irrational.'

'Perhaps.'

'M45 is not a priority.'

'Not for you.'

'Listen, Colin. I don't give a corkscrew chuff box for the budget. It's you I'm bothered about, my friend.'

'Thanks, Owen. I appreciate that. Is R.T. in?'

'Yes.'

'Right. I'll see whether he wants my head on a charger or as it comes.'

Colin left the control room and went to the Director's office. He knocked on the door.

'R.T.?'

'Whisterfield. Come in; you already have. Take a seat. Aren't you on sick leave?'

The Director was his calm self. He turned a stone paper-weight under his hand: the only sign; and the blue of his eyes.

'You're not happy,' said Colin.

'Correct.'

'M45.'

'Precisely.'

'Why?'

'Look here, Whisterfield. You are an able fellow. You have the potential to expand our understanding of the cosmos. Yet you fritter the budget on a cluster of adjacent stellar trinkets that is more the stuff of students.'

'And if it isn't?'

'What are you saying?'

'The fact that M45 is a local phenomenon may be irrelevant.'

'But it is science that others less creative could do.'

'"Creative"? R.T. You built your contraption outside to look for something you never have found. Now it finds what wasn't even guessed at and wouldn't have been discovered without you. Was that only science?'

The Director's hand on the paperweight was still.

'All I ask is a chance,' said Colin.

'I hear you, my boy,' said the Director. 'Watch your back.'

'Thanks,' said Colin, and closed the door behind him.

'And?' said Owen.

'He's fine,' said Colin. 'He understood when I explained what I was doing.'

'Well, I'd not have put money on it, choose what you say,' said Owen. 'Here are the printouts. And you're still sick, lad. Go home.'

'I shall. Oh, and by the bye. The chough, *Pyrrhocorux pyrrhocorux*, builds its nest of twigs, roots and plant stems, lined with grass on cliffs or in old buildings; Slater, Williams and Whisterfield, page 102. It would not, and could not, use a box.'

Colin wheeled his bicycle across the grass to the security fence and looked up at the white dish. It was parked in the zenith. He heard the wind among the struts. A klaxon sounded. The hum of the drive motors started, and the amber warning lights on the bogies flashed. The three thousand tonnes of steel began to move in azimuth and elevation and the red eye of the central focus mast tilted into view. The two towers that held the dish crept along their rails. The note of the wind changed, the stresses of the girders and of the dish made their own music as the telescope tracked, slowed to the measure of the Earth's turning, and the motors died near to silence.

Colin checked. 15.15. He squinted. Azimuth 157·6°; Elevation 58° 20′; Right Ascension 3h. 46′; Declination +24° 11′. Good old Owen.

So the day shrank and night stretched. The clonter of the cobbles in the river was silent, and the river fell to sleep.

Then was the time when day and night were the same, and

the sun tipped towards death. He went to the stack. The bones were clean and the wind had taken the hair to be found when birds built nests again; and the woman and the child were gone into life.

He brought the bones to Ludcruck. He eased them through the grit so they would not break. He reached to the nooks of the dead and lifted aside the old to make way for the new. And when they were quiet he left them.

The sun was dying, but hope would come. He counted as the cold gripped. If hope did not come, the sun would not turn, and there would be nothing but the wanderers, the curving of the stars, winter, and the moon.

At each clear dark he went above Ludcruck to the Bearstone and watched as the Stone Spirit, riding on the Bull's back, the Bull that he had made new with the blade and with his hand, climbed the wall of the night cave. He watched the ring of stars that sat upon the Spirit's brow, and watched until the Bull dropped below the hills.

And at the next dark he watched; and the next. If the Stone Spirit should see there was no one to care that the sun was weak it would not give the fire of its brow and the stars would end. Then where would be beasts to hunt? Where the hunters? Where the Hunter in the sky?

Once, when the world was full, the Hunter walked the sky. Above him was the Bull, and through the nights of winter it went before him with lowered horns. But when the world grew empty the Hunter left to follow the herds; yet the Bull stayed. And every night he rose above the hills. He hooked his red eye over, watching to see that there was life, and the Stone Spirit looked to send out eagles from its head to feed the stars. Then, when they had seen that the world was well and the stars were fed, the Bull and the Stone Spirit rested until night came again.

And each dancer in Ludcruck made new the Bull and the

beasts on the wall of the cave sky for the time when all would be again, with the Hunter striding. But if the dancer did not dance and sing and make new the Bull on the sky wall, the Stone Spirit would not send eagles.

Yet there was a greater than the Bull, a greater than the Stone Spirit; for they kept the world and the stars through winter, but Crane kept through all Time.

Crane flew never resting along the River above the sky. It flew the highmost heavens and drove down upon the night. At deepest winter, when the sun could die, it thrust its beak to the dark above the Tor of Ghosts that lay under the star that did not turn. Then, when it seemed that it must strike the Tor, at the midpoint of the night, Crane skimmed the crest and rose to dive again in everlasting life. So the Bull cared for the world, the Stone Spirit for the stars, Crane for world, stars and the round of Time.

With the woman and the child gone into Ludcruck, he made a snow hole at the Bearstone and sat as the Bull lifted, to show that he kept watch and worked that the world would not be lost. And, as he sat, hope came.

Above the Bull's back the Stone Spirit put up its hand and plucked eagles from the ring about its brow and sent them out. They flew as sparks across the night, gliding on their feathered fire about the cave, and the stars were fed. Every night he watched, until every eagle had flown and the sky was new though the sun sank.

Each year the sun went to die; and each year the Stone Spirit and the eagles fetched it back, though it had its trick to play.

With every setting, the sun drew nearer to death, the point of Moel, the Hill of Night, the hill from which there was no return. And at last it sank, big, into Moel and was gone. Then, if the Stone Spirit had not fed the stars, the sun had died. But now it crept behind the ridge of Moel until it came to the Nick in the hill, and blinked.

15

For three nights the sun played with the world, dying into Moel, and blinking at the Nick. Then it stopped its play, and climbed from Moel and death, so that night shrank and day stretched once more.

Colin locked his bicycle at the Health Centre and twirled the combination. He rubbed disinfectant gel into his hands from the dispenser before tapping his details on the screen. He saw that he was expected and was invited to the waiting area.

He sat and watched the red LED dots cycle their information: welcome, statistics, chiding of appointments missed, a clinic for infant eczema, monitoring of blood pressure, electronic beeps of the summoning of patients to their doctors, please ask a member of staff if you need help.

A woman was reading a book to a child on her knee.

'"So the little boy went into the wood, and he met a witch." Don't pick your nose. "And the witch said, 'You come home with me and I'll give you a good dinner.'" Now you wouldn't go home with a witch, would you?'

'I wouldn't, Nan.'

'But this little boy does. "The witch's house stood on hens' legs." Isn't that daft?'

He nodded.

'"And the witch said, 'Come in, and I'll give you some dinner.'" Would you go in?'

He shook his head.

'Well, the little boy, see, he's going in. "The witch said, 'Come upstairs.'" Would you go upstairs with a witch?'

'Don't go,' said Colin.

The woman looked at him.

'"So the boy went upstairs." If you went upstairs in a witch's house, what would you do?'

'I'd wee.'

Colin stood. 'Young man. Do not go into the witch's house.

16

Do not. And whatever you do, do not go upstairs. You must not go upstairs. Do not go! You are not to go!'

The woman put her arm around the child.

'You must not go upstairs!'

A receptionist came from her desk.

'Professor Whisterfield.'

'You must not go!'

'Professor Whisterfield.'

'He must not go upstairs! I have been upstairs! They are not hens' legs! They are not the legs of hens!'

'Professor Whisterfield. Please.'

'He must not.'

Beep. The LEDs flashed. Colin Whisterfield. Room 5.

'You mustn't. They are not *Gallus gallus domesticus*,' said Colin as he left the waiting area.

'That man's funny,' said the boy. 'He makes me laugh.'

Colin knocked on the open door.

'Hi,' said the doctor. 'How was the hospital?'

'Farce.'

'Do you want to continue?'

'If you like. Don't let that boy go in.'

'Boy?' said the doctor.

'The one outside.'

'Go in where?'

'The witch's house.'

The doctor linked his hands behind his neck, pushed his chair backwards, and spun until it came to rest.

Colin leaned forward and turned the computer screen. 'So what have we here? Well, these cocktails didn't work, did they? That. And that. And that. Oh, I remember that. How I remember that. And that. And that. And as for that! I didn't care. Chemically poleaxed. I'd rather be mad. Give me a healthy psychosis any day.'

'All I can do is offer advice,' said the doctor. 'It's up to you

17

whether you take it. We've exhausted the pharmacopoeia. ECT isn't ideal, but that's where we're at.'

Colin held the screen frame at arm's length and shut his eyes against the facts. He swung his head one way, then the other, and began to shake. The doctor loosened the fingers from the computer. Colin clapped his palms to his face and slouched on the desk.

'Help me.'

The doctor waited.

'There's nowhere. Nowhere to go. I've nowhere. Else.'

'You had to admit it yourself, Colin. It had to come from you. If people get too close you act the goat; and you're so damned clever and devious you run rings round any argument you don't want to hear. You'd run rings round me, if I let you.'

'I can't manage any more.'

'If you mean that, there is somebody you wouldn't con.'

'Alone. Inside. I am so alone.'

'Did you hear what I said?'

'Yes. All right. Yes. Anything. Whatever you want.'

'She's not to everyone's taste; but she gets results.'

Colin looked up. '"She"?'

'Is that a problem for you?'

'Is she a witch?'

'What on earth do you mean? Don't talk such rubbish, man. Of course she isn't a witch. She's a highly qualified psychiatrist and, in my opinion, if you're the least bit concerned, an even better psychotherapist. Colin, sometimes you say the strangest things.'

'She could still be a witch,' said Colin. 'Does she like crows? Carrion crows? *Corvus corone corone*?'

'I've no idea. I haven't asked her.'

'OK,' said Colin. 'OK.'

'What are you talking about?' said the doctor. 'What's bothering you?'

'Nothing. Nothing. It's all right.'

'It clearly is not all right. You've got a tremor.'

'It's nothing. I concur. Just let's stop. This. Please.'

'Leave it with me, then. I'll cancel the hospital.'

'As you wish. Whatever you want.'

'It'll be rough.'

'I understand the implication.'

Colin got up to go.

'Eric.'

'Yes?'

'You were spinning the chair anti-clockwise. That's unlucky. Always turn with the sun.'

The sun worked, and the cold gripped more; but it would pass. He had to travel the White Rocks before the clonter of spring began and the waters blocked his return.

The time came when day and night moved the world from winter. He took a bag of skin and went in the dark to the Bearstone and smelt the wind. It was in the Flatlands, where the sun now set. He watched Crane climb the sky, pulling the day up from below the hills, and as it reached above his head, night became empty of black, Crane faded into the light, and the coming sun hardened the edges of the hills as it rose behind him.

He took the leg bone of a crane from the bag and he went down into Ludcruck and faced the wall of the bird spirits. He danced the day and put the bone to his lips and played. He played the cranes from their sleep. The bone made their cry, and the cry answered from the spirit wall and joined with the sound, growing, back and to, back and to, so that his playing was lost in the greater cry. He stopped, but the sound went on, until all Ludcruck was a waking of cranes.

Over the Flatlands black lines and dabs rose in the sky cave, swirling, bulls, shifting, hinds, horses, antlers, horns, haunches as the cranes rose, wheeled and firmed into heads of spears.

He danced in the sound, and the sound of Ludcruck was loud and louder as the cranes flew above. He danced and he danced. He danced to join them. The spear shadows darkened. He danced. He danced his spirit wings, and lifted out of the rock into the company of the birds.

The cranes flew beyond the Bearstone, and he with them. His legs lay behind, his head stretched before, and his throat called. He flew in the spearheads over the Black Peaks towards the White Rocks, and across the White Rocks, by ridges and ice and down to the Lower Lands where the pines grew; on and on, calling, calling in the gale of feathers, through the day, until the Valley of Life showed.

Strength left him. The Valley was his journey. The cranes flew above, but he sank beneath, and his voice lost the music of the greater cry; and with the last beat of his wings he came to the edge of a crag and was a man.

Colin built momentum to above Beacon Lodge so that he freewheeled from there. The gradient as far as the lay-by at Castle Rock could be cancelled by the wind. It depended on the camber, and cars blared at him as he wobbled to the crest of the Front Hill; but he made it and began the drop past Armstrong Farm.

'Down in Pennsyltucky where the pencils grow
There's a little spot I think you ought to know.
'Tis a place, no doubt, you've never heard about;
It isn't on the map, I do declare.
It's a spot they call the Imazaz,
Nestling itself among the hills.
'Twas there I learnt my prayer.
'Twas there I learnt to swear.
'Twas there I took my first two Beecham's pills,

Ta-rah-rah!'

He passed the notice at Whinsbrow. THIS HILL IS STILL DANGEROUS. Straight down from Rockside to the five-lane-ends and the roundabout.

'There's a cottage so sweet
At the end of the street,
And it's Number Ninety-Four.
Oh, I'm going back to Imazaz:
Imazaz a pub next door!'

At the bottom he braked to lessen momentum, so that by leaning hard over and trailing his foot he cleared the round-about and veered right into London Road and the traffic. He worked among the flocks of cars. They all had black glass in the windows. Then the station approach made him pedal. Two point zero four kilometres; approximately.

After the station he went by Brook Lane and Row-of-Trees, urging past Lindow Moss, along Seven Sisters Lane to Toft. The house stood at the end of a drive, among rhododendrons. He lodged his bicycle and rang the doorbell.

'Whisterfield. Colin Whisterfield.'

'Do come in, Professor Whisterfield. Doctor Massey is expecting you.'

The entrance corridor had a side room.

'Please wait here.'

Colin waited.

He waited.

'Doctor Massey is ready now, Professor.'

He was led into a bigger room, lined with books. French windows opened to lawns. A woman lay on a chaise longue, reading a file. She wore a suit of dark silk. 'Hi,' she said, without looking up.

'You're quite young,' said Colin.

'"Quite".'

'Your hair's black.'

'That's this week, darling. Tomorrow may be a different story.'

There was a diamond-paned cabinet. The tumblers and decanter inside were of crystal.

'Are you looking for a drink?' she said.

'May I? Is it allowed?'

'No. But there's ice and water over there. Help yourself.'

'Thanks.'

'Cheers,' she said, and continued her reading.

Colin scanned the books. 'You have a fascinating library. Eclectic.'

'Yes, I have.'

'I could make myself a tome here. That's a pun; which is a play on words to exploit ambiguities and innuendoes in their meaning, usually for humorous effect.'

'Oh, ha-bloody-ha. Sit down.'

Colin sat in a deep leather chair on the other side of the marble fireplace from the chaise longue. By the chair there was a low table on casters, and an open box of tissues. He was facing the windows. The chaise longue and the woman were silhou-ettes, the light on the silk picking out her form.

Colin held the tumbler in both hands and drank.

She shut the file, swung her legs round and sat forward. Pendant earrings broke the light, and her eyes were violet green.

'And—Action. You're Colin. I'm Meg. What's up?'

'I—'

A clock ticked. There were crystal chandeliers.

'Do you like crows?' he said.

'I can take 'em or leave 'em.'

'I—'

'"I" what?'

Colin drank again.

'I—don't know.'

'Well, I'm buggered if I do,' she said.

'I—'

22

Colin emptied the tumbler. 'What am I supposed to say?'

'What do you want to say?'

'I—'

'Where's the pain?'

'I don't understand,' said Colin.

'So why have you come? Because you're in pain. Right? Something hurts. Right? Go there.'

'Go where?'

'Go to where the pain is most and say what it tells you.'

'Tells me what?'

'Holy macaroli. Spare me the smart-arses. We're not talking the square root of minus one.'

'That's i,' said Colin. 'i's imaginary.'

'Is you indeed?' said Meg. 'Is that a fact? Oh, switch your sodding brains off. Don't think. Feel.'

'How?'

'He says "How?" How? Ask it. It hurts, too. It wants to tell you.'

'"It",' said Colin. 'What's "it"?'

'Search me.'

Colin looked at the tumbler. The tumbler flashed. He looked around. The diamond glass. Light. Blue silver. He looked up. The chandeliers. Lightning.

'Can't. Can't. Nothing. It's—'

Her earrings. Blue, silver. Blue silvers. Lightnings.

'—No!'

He stood, smashed the tumbler on the marble and fell back, curled, his arms covering his head. The blaze from the fragments lanced his mind. He roared. He screamed. The howl tore his chest, and ran to wordless snatches of sound. She leaned forward and passed him the box of tissues.

'I'm sorry,' said Colin. 'I'm sorry. I'm so sorry. I am so sorry.'

'There's nothing to be sorry for, Sunny Jim. It's those question-begging reductive pharmaceutical plonkers that should be sorry.

They've put you through the wringer. They've even fried your head. Or tried to. Eric suggested ECT? I'm surprised. Good job you stopped. But that's spilt milk. Someone should have read this file before it got to me.'

'What happens next?'

'You go home,' she said.

'Go home. Yes. Go. Home. But then. I've only just come.'

'You've been on the road to here for a long time, Colin, and you've had a trashing now. You need to settle. Same time next week? Sooner, if you want. Or not at all?'

'Next week. Home. Thanks.'

'You're welcome.'

'I'm—'

'Mm?' She put her feet up on the chaise longue.

'I'm not being—difficult—on purpose.'

'Who's saying you're difficult?'

He left the room, to the corridor, out, and was sick into the rhododendrons.

Colin lifted his bicycle, but could not ride. He pushed it. The traffic, the black windows. Trucks to and from the M6, so high that they were not a part of the world, but blocks moving. He walked on the verge and turned to Seven Sisters Lane.

Here was quiet. Colin sat astride the saddle, and fell, retching. The spasm stopped. He tried again. He had balance. His legs moved. The need to pedal sucked air to his lungs and worked his heart, and by the time he came to Lindow he felt the chill off the Moss. The pull of Brook Lane parched his mouth, leaving the taste of bile on the skin. But he had to walk the Front Hill and rest at Castle Rock lay-by. His empty stomach spewed more bitterness. The road here was too loud for him. He walked, still quivering.

Colin reached the trees and the peace of the quarry, went to the hut and pumped water into a bowl. He rinsed his mouth and cleaned his teeth. Then he washed his hair, and the crusts of vomit from his beard, laid the fire and filled the lamp. He took a box from a shelf and opened it. Inside were layers of paper smelling of cedarwood mothballs.

Colin removed the layers, one by one. Between, there was folded clothing. He lifted each piece and placed it on the table, and when the box was empty he stood back and considered.

'Full dress? Or habit? Convocation? Convocation habit. Con-voc-ation. I think so.'

He put on a white shirt and white bow tie, pulling the ends level. Next the white bands, to hang evenly. He changed his sandals and jeans for black shoes, socks and charcoal grey suit, adjusting the braces so that the trousers broke at the shoe. He fitted gold cufflinks and held the sleeves as he slid his arms into the black gown. Then he brushed the scarlet and blue silk chimere, fitted it over the gown, and fastened it with the two buttons. To finish, Colin slipped the green silk hood with the gold edge over his shoulders and set the bonnet on his head, and adjusted the tassel.

He checked in the mirror, arranged his hair and beard. He locked the hut and made his way from the quarry to the track, holding up the gown and chimere to avoid snagging. He turned left.

Away to the right were the hills: the flat top of the cone of Shuttlingslow stood clean and in the freshness he saw farms and fields on its lower slopes. To the south was Sutton with its tower. Colin went along the old broad way by Seven Firs and Goldenstone to the barren sand and rocks on Stormy Point and Saddlebole and looked out across the plain beneath. Kinder's table was streaked with the last of late snow; Shining Tor was black.

Colin stood, pulled his hood about him, and breathed the wind. He saw the bright of spring. He smelt returning life. Then, in a moment that he knew, it was time to go. The Edge was waking to its other self. He turned from Stormy Point and strode back through the woods along the broad way.

He sat outside in the evening light with a bottle of wine.

'I am. Must. Am.'

Colin sat, watching the shadows move over the herringbone pick marks on the wall of dimension stone. And when he could see the marks no more he went into the hut, and without lighting lamp or fire, undressed, folded the clothes into their box, got into the bunk and cried himself to sleep.

He lay for one day. He lay for two days. He lay for three days. He woke and blew a fire heap.

'Afternoon.'

'Hi, Trouble,' said Owen. 'You're looking rough.'

'Thanks. Can't think why,' said Colin.

'Rough as old gorse. What's up? Has your mother sold her mangle?'

'This lot.' He dumped a wedge of paper in the waste bin. 'God, the kids are bad today.'

'I've learnt to tune 'em out.'

'We should get those dishes moved. Create an idiot zone.'

'You've got a right cob on, haven't you?' said Owen.

'Sorry. Could you run these data, to see if there's anything fresh? No hurry. Tomorrow will do.' Colin slid a notebook across the control desk.

'And here's the latest for you to look at while you're badly,' said Owen.

'Thanks. I'll take them to my pillow.' Colin unfolded the first sheets and scanned them.

Dill doule.

'What? What did you say?'

'Colin, we've been too long at this lark—'

'*Alauda arvensis arvensis*. It flies high and is insectivorous,

26

with an exuberant song carried out on the wing. There's also a liquid trilling flight note; Slater, Williams and Whisterfield, page 208. Sorry. You were saying. M45.'

'As heck as like. I was saying you're off sick, you should be at home, and if this bollocks you're gobbing is part of it—'

'All's well,' said Colin. 'Please don't lose any sleep over me. Apart from the hardware, I can drudge from home as easily as here.' He put the new sheets into his backpack. 'Now I'm going to sort those kids.'

He went out past the Discovery Centre over the grass. There was a notice: WHISPERING DISHES. Two metal bowls stood apart from the telescope, inconspicuous against its presence, but the same parabolic shape. They were mounted on edge, facing each other. The focal point of each was a central ring held on three struts, and on the rings was engraved SPEAK OR LISTEN HERE, and there were two aluminium steps up to the rings, with rails on either side. Children were swinging on the stabilising frame at the back, labelled PLEASE DO NOT CLIMB ON THIS SUPPORT STRUCTURE. Other children were on the steps of both dishes, yelling across the gap, and others running and barging at each other between. Colin went close, saying nothing, waited. The noise died under his presence.

'It doesn't work if you shout,' he said. 'You must whisper. Softly. Otherwise the signal distorts. And if you face away from the dish it's forty-one point seven metres between, and all you hear is your own voice. You have to turn towards the dish and whisper into the ring. Then the person at the other end can hear you. Try it. Like this. Excuse me.' Colin stood at the foot of the steps, held the rails and whispered into the focus ring. 'Hello?'

The children had drifted off. There was one boy and a girl left. 'Go and put your ear at the ring of that dish and listen,' Colin said to the girl.

The girl ran, and when she was in position he said to the boy, 'You stand up and speak into the ring as I did.'

The boy went to the top step.

'Hello!'

'Too loud. You have to remember to whisper,' said Colin. 'The parabolic surface has the property that all sound waves disseminate parallel to its central axis and travel the same distance to get to its focus. Which means that the sound bounces off the dish and converges towards the opposite focus in phase, with its pressure peaks and troughs synchronised so that they work together to make the loudest possible sound vibrations. The sound is thus enhanced at the focus, but only if it originates from the source you're aiming it at. It's simple. Radio waves are no different. The telescope operates on the same principle. Try again.'

'Hello!'

'Come down,' said Colin. 'Listen.' He whispered. 'Hello? Can you hear me?'

'Yes!'

'No. Shh. Shh. Like this. Can you hear me?'

There was a giggle at the focus.

'That's it,' said Colin. 'Hello.'

'Hello.'

'Good. Now say something.'

Giggle.

'Shall I say something?'

'Yes.'

'Right. I'll sing you a song. But quietly. Shh. Ready?'

'Yes.'

'Oh, I'm one of the nuts from Barcelona. Did you hear that?'

'Yes.'

'I plink-a-ti-plonk.

I Casa-bi-onk.'

More nervous laughter. Colin held the rails and danced, kicking his legs out, keeping his mouth at the focus. The boy ducked and crouched by the steps.

'Round at de bar I order wine-o.
Half de mo I'm feeling fine.
Light-a de fag, de old Woodbine-o.
Order de cab for half-past nine.
I'm one of the nuts from Barcelona.
I plink-a-ti-plonk.
I Casa-bi-onk.
Did you like that?'

Silence.

'Another try,' said Colin. 'Remember. Whisper. Whisper. Shh. Hello.'

'Hello.'

'Perfect. Great. That's the way to do it.'

'Hello, Col.'

'What?'

'Where've you been all this while?'

'What?'

'You know.'

'You? Is it you?'

'Who else?'

He turned. There was no one at the dish. The girl was playing with the others.

'You!'

There was no answer.

'Don't go! Don't leave me again!'

The Valley of Life was safe, but under the ice he heard the first waters. He could not stay.

Colin stumbled between the dishes, calling, listening, calling, calling. There was only ambient sound. He sat on the steps, his head in his hands, past tears.

'Professor Whisterfield.'

One of the staff of the Discovery Centre had come out to him.

'What, Gwen?'

'I'd like a word with you. You're all right, son,' she said to the boy, who was peering through the treads.

'He's bloody mad! He wants locking up! I'll tell me mam!'

'You do that. Now off. Go on. Imshi. Pronto. Vamoose. Scoot. Shoo. Skedaddle.'

The boy ran.

'Colin, what the hell do you think you're at?'

'Survival.'

'We can't afford this.'

'Me neither.'

'Inside, and no messing.'

Colin stood and walked with her, back to the Centre. He held her sleeve between finger and thumb. She took him to her office and sat him down.

'Sorry, Gwen.'

'"Sorry" won't do, Colin. Any more of that and there could be a shitstorm.'

'"Bonkers boffin bloodies blockhead beef-wits"?'

'Shut your trap and get off site. You're not supposed to be here. You and the other barmpots, you think you own the place.'

'But I must be here. I have to be here.'

'Well, I'm telling you straight. You're useless. Nothing but a frigging nuisance. If I see you near my patch again your feet won't touch the ground.'

He took moss and blew a brand at the fire heap and went down, swinging the brand to keep its flame.

Between the river and the crags there were no lodges nor any sign of being. He broke dead branches from fallen trees and went to a cave. He called, but only the rock spirit answered. He looked around at the earth and the floor. No one had sat here. No one had passed by. There were bones with cut marks, but they were old, gnawed by wolves and beasts and long ago. Earth covered the ashes.

He walked from cave to cave of the Valley of Life until the last. It was thin. He made a torch of pine, moved into the gap and eased himself along. The way grew wider, and there was a place where a hearth had been, but nothing now. He moved on. The passage closed again, and he came to people; but beasts had splintered their bones and cast them about, and no one had come back to care; nor were any of them new. And beyond the people there were the bones of cranes, and the cave end.

He went back to the light and the sky. He looked across the Valley to the other shore and the cave there. He had to go.

He stepped over the ice.

The cave faced the star that did not turn, and he sat at the cave mouth through the day and sang the sun along until night filled with black and the sky River ran into the cave of bones, then lifted above the crags so that Crane could fly. He sang Crane round from its lowmost up to its height to bring the day. And when he saw that the sun had woken he made the fire heap strong and lit the pine, stood, and went to the cave.

He entered the chamber and raised the torch to the bird cut nesting in the roof. He saw it, and its eye saw him. He passed the slots of women, which made the tracks of birds, along the walls and by beasts that he knew in Ludcruck.

He left the cave, into a passage to where he had to crawl, to the place of the Dark and of the Woman. She had no head, but her breasts were rumps, and her legs were two cranes plunging.

There was nowhere else for him, nothing else to do. He had to reach the life within her. He slid his hand along the necks into the cleaving. He felt. He drew his hand out from the wall. His fingers were dry. There was no blood. The rock was dead.

Wolf! Wolf! Grey Wolf! I am calling for you!

Far away the Grey Wolf heard, and came.

Here am I, the Grey Wolf.

There is no one to be; no one to give my flesh to the air, to take my bones to the cliff and the nooks of the dead. No one shall cut the bulls. No one shall watch. The Stone Spirit shall not send eagles. The stars must end. The sun must die. Crane shall fly alone. All shall be winter the wanderers and the moon.

That is not Trouble. The Trouble is yet to come. Sit up on me, the Grey Wolf.

He sat up on the shoulder. The Grey Wolf struck the damp earth and ran, higher than the trees, lower than the clouds, and each leap measured a mile; from his feet flint flew, spring spouted, lake surged and mixed with gravel dirt, and birch bent to the ground. Hare crouched, boar bristled, crow called, owl woke, and stag began to bell. And the Grey Wolf stopped.

They were in Ludcruck at the wall of the bird spirits. The skin bag was before him, and a crane bone lay beside.

Get down from me, the Grey Wolf. Cut. Dance. Sing. Bring. Do not forget.

How shall I cut dance sing bring and not forget when the end is nothing?

Long hair, short wit. I, the Grey Wolf, am speaking. Do it. I come three times. No more.

The Grey Wolf struck the damp earth and was gone.

'Hello. This is Colin Whisterfield. May I speak to Doctor Massey, please?'

'Can I take a message, Professor?'

'No. I'm afraid not. I must speak to her. Now.'

'Please hold.'

'Hi, Colin.'

'Meg. I need to see you. Today.'

'Well, that was quick. Of course you can.'

'What time?'

'Whenever. Take care.'

'Hello. Is that High Forest Taxis?'

'It is indeed, Professor Whisterfield.'

'I have to go from Alderley to Toft. Now. As soon as possible. And I'd like the driver to be Bert. He knows where I am. Thanks. Thanks very much. You're so kind.'

He left the quarry for the road and paced until the taxi came.

'Eh up, Colin. Are you all right? What's it today, then?' said Bert. 'The nut house?'

'It's not as far as Barcelona.'

'No worries.' Colin sat in the front. Bert whistled as he drove, and kept winking at Colin. They turned onto the drive. Meg was by the house, lopping holly branches.

'Hi, Colin. Hi, Bert.'

'Hi, Doc,' said Bert.

'Go in, Colin,' said Meg. 'I'll stow the gear and be with you.'

'Watch them gullantines, Doc,' said Bert, 'else they'll have you.'

Colin went to the library and looked out over the lawns.

'I didn't know you knew Bert,' he said.

'Bert and I go back a long way.'

Only, in all the world, he entered the lodge.

'Am I mad?' said Colin.

'Not yet,' said Meg.

'But a voice. That's psychosis.'

'Depends on the voice,' said Meg. 'Have you heard it before?'

'No.'

'Did you recognise it?'

'Yes.'

'A real person?'

'—Yes.'

'You don't sound too sure.'

'I think,' said Colin.

'Oh, you "think",' said Meg. 'Now. Let's unpick this. You hear

33

a voice you've not heard before, and you "think" it's the voice of someone you recognise. Dead or alive?'

'I don't know. I don't know. I don't know. I don't know. I don't know. I must find her.'

'You just hold your water. So it's a "she".'

'Yes.'

'How can you tell? A whisper is voiceless. Hard to differentiate.'

'She calls me Col. No one else does. No one else knows. It's just between the two of us. At secret times.'

'"Did" or "does"? "Knew" or "knows"?'

'Does. Knows.'

'So it's all in the present.'

'It depends on whether time is linear,' said Colin.

'Who is she? Was she?'

Colin began to cry.

'Who, Colin?'

'My sister.'

'What's her name?'

'I—can't remember.'

Meg took Colin by the hand.

'Come up, love. Come up.'

She helped him from the chair and walked him across the room to the French windows.

'I'm sorry,' he said. 'I never cry.'

'Why not? I do. Does me a world of good. You're always apologising. Stop. Let it go. You're OK. Let it go.'

They stood, hand in hand, looking at the sunlit gardens of spring. Wrench by wrench Colin's tears turned to dew on his cheeks.

'What's that rock over there?' he said.

The distant flat horizon was broken by a bluff.

'Beeston,' said Meg. 'Shall we start now?'

'Start what?'

'Scraping off the crud.' She took him back to the chair, sat herself opposite and opened his file. 'This is the most God-awful collection of tunnel-visioned codswallop I've seen in all my born puff. There's not a trace of insight, imagination, flexibility, humanity, humility in it. Apart from Eric. It's you that has to conform to the preconceptions of others, and when you don't you're closed down with dope to make you go away. Wuthering dry wankers. They don't want to learn. I'm being unprofessional, of course. You understand.'

'What does it say?' said Colin.

'What doesn't it? About the only thing missing is athlete's foot.'

'Oh, I have that,' said Colin. 'I have that, too. *Tinia pedis*. In summer, by and large, or when using occluded footwear for long periods. I treat it symptomatically. I wash the affected part first and dry it well; then either spray with a fungicide, avoiding inhalation and the eyes, or I can use a cream, twice daily; usually a miconazole nitrate base. It's important to continue the treatment for ten days after the symptoms have disappeared, to prevent them from coming back.'

'That's true,' said Meg. 'Most people do stop too soon. Shall we go on?'

'Yes, of course,' said Colin. 'But it can be a most aggressive itch.'

'It can. Meanwhile, back at the ranch,' said Meg, 'as far as there is a consensus, it's that you're an immature uncooperative hysterical depressive Asperger's, with an IQ off the clock, for what that's worth; which is zilch unless you use it.'

'I can't help being intelligent,' said Colin. 'I'm not contagious.'

'But that's what scares them: the IQ. Makes them defensive and aggressive at the same time. The pack turns on the outsider. Eric says you play games if you think anyone's getting too close. You tried it on with me as soon as we met, as well as now.

Some of this, then, could be you farting about. Or are you? If it was as easy as that we could tank you up and all live happily ever after. But you would not. Cutting your emotional balls off would solve nothing. Colin, has no one spotted the truly weird part of you?'

'What's that?'

'Your tail feathers. They're grotesque.'

He looked behind him. 'There aren't any.'

'Oh, come on. That doesn't wash with me. Concentrate, will you? MA, M.Sc. Clever boy. D.Phil. Fine. D.Sc. Right. FRS, FRAS. Congratulations. M.Theol. A bit *de trop* for an astrophysicist? Then, perhaps not.'

'It takes two lines to get your qualifications on an envelope,' said Colin.

'My inferiority complex,' said Meg. 'Nothing to write home about. But you, matey, you're something else. What's this truckload of Masters'? Archaeology and Anthropology? Geography? Geology? What's going on? It's barmy. How's your sex life?'

'That's not important.'

'Does the thought make you puke?'

'No. I've got colleagues. They're good colleagues.'

'Have you talked to any of them about this?' said Meg.

'They wouldn't understand what's wrong. They don't think anything is. They don't know what it's like. Inside. For them it's only fun, even though I tell them it isn't. You see, I don't delete. Anything. Ever.'

'Are you saying you've got an eidetic memory?' said Meg.

'My colleagues think I have,' said Colin. 'But it's not that I don't delete. I can't delete. I can't delete. Not even dreams.'

'Oh, heck,' said Meg. 'What were you doing at half past eleven on the evening of November 7th two years ago?'

'Arthur's tracking an anomaly near 24 Tauri for me, and I'm supervising some postgrad researchers with the Mark II on the Taurids maximum at Right Ascension 53° Declination +24°.'

'Who's Arthur?'

'The main computer for the telescope.'

'And what about noon on January 14th thirteen years ago?'

'I'm splitting logs. A Scots pine blew down in the night of January 11th.'

'Who was President of the United States then?'

'I don't know.'

'What won the Grand National two years ago?'

'I don't know.'

'Where were the last Olympic Games held?'

'Sorry.'

'What did you do in the afternoon three days after your sixteenth birthday?'

'Double Latin. Double. I ask you! It's a set text. *The Aeneid*, Book Six, lines 703 to 751. It's too much to expect anyone of our age to take in all of that at the one go. I want to hide. I'm frightened. I'm no good at it, and I don't understand. Then Maths. Calculus. Infinite Series Convergence. Then we go for a cross-country run. I come fifth. Tea's Welsh rarebit and cake with chocolate buttons on. I have two pieces.'

'OK. You're not a savant,' said Meg. 'Your recall seems to be totally autobiographical, and we must assume totally accurate.'

'That's right,' said Colin. 'It is.'

'Press on,' said Meg. 'What was the weather when you were twelve years nine months three weeks and six days old?'

Colin thrust his face against a cushion and gagged. 'No! No! Sky gone! Eyes! Old! Old eyes! Strong! Blue light! Silver! No! Gone!'

Meg waited. Colin flexed and slumped. He lifted his face from the cushion. 'I don't know,' he said. 'You see. That's it. You see. I can't access anything, anything, before I was thirteen.'

'Oh, twice and double heck,' said Meg. 'You don't present this way in the file. Haven't you told anyone?'

'I've tried,' said Colin. 'But no one listens. Or I'm not clear. I suppose I'm too scared.'

'So you should be.'

'Of going mad.'

'You are not going mad. Yet. Let's work arsy-varsy. You can't remember anything before you were thirteen, right? Is that what you're saying?'

'I get flashbacks,' said Colin. 'But they don't connect. They don't add up to being me. It's as if they're teasing on purpose. They're cruel. Him! His eyes!'

'So you've no autonoetic awareness of yourself as a continuous entity across time.'

'I don't. That's it, Meg. I can't access the data. Not at will, I can't. That's it.'

'I'm not so sure it is it,' said Meg. 'Episodic memory and isolated retrograde amnesia are rare enough. But this may be another ball game.'

'What are you going to do?' said Colin.

'Me? I'm not going to do anything. You're the one that has to do. Now then. Once you've had a flashback from your forgotten past, are those images retained and retrievable in the present?'

'Yes.'

'Are you able to remember dreams as flashback?'

'I think I can. But I can't be sure whether they're dreams or something else that actually happened.'

'Mm. Okey-dokey. Well. There's a handful of case studies of your other syndrome of autobiographical total memory, and some ambitious people are trying to build their reputations on it. Hyperthymesia; makes it sound kosher. They may be right. But I'm not having you dragged in. You don't know these careerists. They're bent on being first, and they wouldn't see; or if they did some wouldn't care. On top of that, if hyperthymesia turns out to be genuine, which it well may, you could have both syndromes, butt-jointing at some time when you were about thirteen. And that, Humpty Dumpty, O best belovèd, would be dynamite to blow you apart. And all the king's horses and all the king's men. I'm flummoxed. This could be unique. I'd not wish uniqueness on anyone.'

'What's the answer?' said Colin.

'Squit all, at the moment,' said Meg. 'You have flashback from your forgotten period, and those images are retained and retrievable.'

'Yes.'

'So why did you smash the glass, Colin?'

'No.'

'Why did you smash the glass?'

'No.'

'Why did you?'

'No!'

'OK. We've shovelled enough shit for one day. Let's sleep on it. I want you to have an MRI brain scan.'

'Not hospital,' said Colin. 'I mustn't leave home. I have to be there.'

'It's a morning trip to Macclesfield, non-invasive, no after-effects; and it might tell us more.'

'Will Bert look after me?'

'I'm sure he will. Let's have a breather, and I'll show you something that might interest you. Come into the corridor.'

'I'm feeling so much better,' said Colin.

'Don't worry. It's a transient euphoria.'

They went from the library to the corridor. The corridor ran straight through the house, from front to back. 'Look over the lawn,' said Meg. Beeston bluff was in the centre of the view. 'At the winter solstice, the sun sets towards the hill, almost.'

'"Almost"?' said Colin.

'It goes down to the left, by that bush, and when the sky's clear Beeston stands out a short while later, as if there's a fire behind it.'

Colin held his thumb sideways and closed one eye. 'About ten thousand years ago it would have set exactly there. This corridor could echo an earlier significance.'

'Oh Gawd. Are you into ley lines?' said Meg.

'No, but it may be, it may be, that this place could have been used for solar and lunar observations.'

'Well, it has good vibes,' said Meg. 'Anyway. Time to go now.'

'Will it be inconvenient if I wait till Bert gets here?' said Colin.

'I think you'll find he's outside.'

Colin went to the front door. The taxi was on the drive; and Bert was reading a paper.

'Have I kept you waiting?' said Colin.

'Part of the service,' said Bert. 'Are you all right? Let's be having you.'

Colin lowered the window. 'I've got to find her. I've got to.'

'Take care,' said Meg.

'Do you always say that?'

'Not always.' She waved as they started to move away.

'Our Meg,' said Bert. 'She's an odd un, that one. She is and all. What! She reckons you up, rump and stump, she does. Rump and stump. What! But she sees you right.'

'How long have you known her?' said Colin.

'Meg? Oh, as long as me arm.'

They came to Church Quarry. 'I have to go to hospital,' said Colin. 'You will be able to collect me and bring me back, won't you?'

'Part of the service. But let's have you in here first.' He went with Colin to the hut.

'Thank you,' said Colin. 'I really do appreciate your kindness.'

'Any time,' said Bert.

Colin put on his robes and walked the woods.

*

The woods opened summer. Pine, birch, juniper, willow. He went down the length of two days' hunting into the valleys. He found no one, nor any sign of a one, to the start of the Flatlands. Then he looked for three days' hunting in the hills away from the Tor of Ghosts but found no one, nor any sign of a one. So he went up towards the Tor and the land of the star that did not turn.

He met spirits on the high fell; wolves, too, and bulls, and bears and boars, but of people he found no one, nor any sign of a one. He climbed the Tor and looked out across all that was; and he saw nothing. He went back to his lodge, and wept; but he did not forget.

Bert was prompt.

'Grand day for it, Colin,' he said. 'Are you all right? Let's be having you.' Colin sat at the front. 'I was thinking. A grand day. Though we'll get a rinsing before we've done. When you can see the rocks on Shining Tor it promises wet.'

'Do you mind if I ask a question?' said Colin.

'Shoot, Prof.'

'I rang your office, and the manager knew who I was without my saying. How was that?'

'She's got a memory for voices, has our Fay,' said Bert.

'But I'd not spoken to her before,' said Colin. 'The hospital made the call.'

'We look after our customers,' said Bert.

'And your milometer isn't working. It doesn't change.'

'I'd best get it fixed.'

'But, if you don't know how far you've gone, how can you manage your fares?'

'When you've been at it a while,' said Bert, 'you know how much it costs.'

The taxi stopped at the main entrance of the hospital. Colin checked in at the desk and went to the waiting area. 'Professor

Whisterfield? This way, please.' The nurse was gentle. 'Now, I want you to go into the booth and take everything off, including your watch, and put this gown on. Your details are here, but I have to be sure that you're not wearing a pacemaker and that you have no other metal on or in your body. Right?' He put on the gown, and the nurse took him to the room. There was a large tube, a tunnel, and at one end a padded bench.

'Lie down here, please, Colin. Are you bothered by being closed in?'

'As far as I'm aware,' said Colin, 'I am not claustrophobic. At least I believe I'm not. I feel enclosed sometimes, in dreams. On my shins. But that's all.'

'Good,' said the nurse. 'You won't go in that far. Now I want you to hold this bulb, and if you're at all worried you're to squeeze it, and we'll stop. And remember. We can hear you and speak to you at all times. During the scan there'll be quite a lot of noise as the magnets switch on and off. Some people find this distressing, so we've got earplugs for you. Or you can listen to music.'

'Thank you,' said Colin. 'I'm interested in the procedure. If it's all the same to you, I'd rather do without.'

'That's fine, Colin. Now I'm going to put this frame over your head, but you'll be able to see clearly. All right? If you'll make yourself comfortable, we'll start. It's important that you don't move. I want you to keep perfectly still.'

The nurse left to join the radiographer behind a window at the end of the room. The bench was raised and slid into the tube, until Colin's head was inside. A voice spoke.

'Can you hear me, Colin?'

'Yes.'

'Then, if you're ready, we'll begin. Remember, we can hear you and speak to you. Try to keep quite still. We're starting. The noise will be loud, so don't hesitate to say if it's too much.'

'Understood,' said Colin.

The bench moved into the tube. There was light, and the curve closed over him. A pause, and then he was lapped in clanging, calling sound. The sound stopped. It came again. It was a sound that pierced. And stopped. And came again. He felt himself a part of its din.

'Good heavens.'

'What's the matter, Colin?'

'Nothing. Nothing.'

'Are you all right?'

'Yes. Please continue.'

The call rang in the tunnel and became him, so he could not tell which was him, the cry, the tunnel. 'It is. *Grus grus.*'

'What, Colin?'

'*Grus grus.*'

'Do you want to come out?'

'No. Go on. *Grus grus.* The common crane.'

'That's fine. Relax.'

'*Grus grus. Grus grus.*'

He closed his eyes. Although he did not move he flew, and the tunnel was a turning sky with stars, five-pointed, red; against his lids. His legs stretched, his throat held the calling; and Time was still.

'We've finished, Colin. You've done very well. We're bringing you out now.'

He did not want it to end. He floated in the night and was one with stars and birds. 'Don't stop. Don't stop the music.'

'Don't worry. I'm here, Col. I'm not leaving you.'

The bench slid back. He opened his eyes. The tube passed, and the nurse was standing by. She lifted the cover from his head. 'Lie there a moment, Colin. That racket can make you dizzy; and we have to check the scan. But you were very good. I thought you'd dropped off to sleep. It's surprising how it affects different people sometimes.'

'Oh, where? Where are you? Tell me.'

'I'm here, Colin. You can get dressed and go home now. Give me your hand, and we'll ring for your taxi.'

Each year he sang and danced in Ludcruck and cut between the worlds to make the beasts free and bring their spirits from behind the rock so that they could spread across the land. And in winter he watched the Bull climb the wall of the sky cave and the Stone Spirit riding to send out eagles to feed the stars. All this he did, though it brought no woman. But every year the sun turned, because of the dance.

Colin rolled the empty oil drum along the floor of the quarry to the hut. He went back and rolled another. He brought out a notebook, callipers, a flexible rule and a pair of dividers, and put them on the table. He tipped the first drum upright and set it level and fixed rocks about it to hold it steady. Then he lifted a stone in both hands and, using it as a maul, began to beat the flat top, moving round the rim and inwards, depressing the surface with dimples. The banging echoed on the rocks.

Round and round he went, so that the metal bent evenly without rupturing the join to the rim. The head of the drum became a dish. He dropped the maul and picked up a mallet and continued round, smoothing the dimples and working the middle down so that the dishing grew steeper. When it was the right depth he took a soft-faced ball-peen hammer and worked more gently, removing the irregularities, making the skin smooth.

He looked at his notes, and measured the hollow, checking with the callipers and marking points with the dividers. Next, he scored a line about the side of the drum, keeping one leg of the dividers against the rim. He lifted the drum, laid it down and worked along the line with mallet and a blunt chisel, driving slots, until with a single knock the top was free. He took it and threw it onto a fire of pallets he had stacked, and he sat and drank water from a can while the fire died.

He pulled the drum head from the ashes and quenched it, and when it had cooled he sat on the ground with it between his legs, read his notes and scored more lines inside the dish with callipers and dividers, turning, checking, turning, checking.

He linked a piezo tuner to the rim and went on tapping.

'Da-di-dum, ti-dum-ti-dumti—' He tapped to the readings of the tuner. '—Dove an-drò senza il mio ben?—' The metal showed the physics of the scoring. The lines drew together as they ought. The maths was right '—Io son pu-re, il tuo fedel-e —' So elegant. '—Rum-ti-titi-pom-ti. Rum-ti-titi-pomti. Ti-pom-ti!'

Colin sat and looked at what he had done. The quarry was quiet.

A noise broke in. He twisted towards the entrance. It was the sound of a machine, an engine, coughing and struggling over the ground. A motorbike appeared at the entrance, black, with high handlebars, black, and the rider was all in black leathers, gauntlets, helmet and visor. It came towards him across the quarry floor. Colin hugged the drum and shuffled away.

'No.'

It came nearer.

'No.'

It stopped. The rider cut the engine, and a gauntlet lifted the visor.

'Hi,' said Meg.

'What are you doing here? What do you want?'

'I did ring, sweetie, but you weren't answering. I thought I'd check out your lair. Have I disturbed you?'

'No. No,' said Colin. 'I don't like surprises, that's all. Sorry.'

'Don't apologise. How many times do I have to say it?'

'Sorry,' said Colin. He got up. 'Please come in.'

Meg dismounted, took off the helmet and shook her hair.

45

'What are you at?' she said.

'I'm making two parabolic dishes. Do come in.'

They went to the hut.

Meg looked around. 'Hey, this is something else.'

'Would you like tea?'

'Thanks.'

'Earl Grey or Lapsang Souchong?'

'I'll pass on the scented muck. Plain builder's with milk, if you have it,' said Meg. 'And no sugar.'

'I think I can do that,' said Colin.

He lit a Primus stove and filled a kettle.

'Bert told me there wasn't electricity,' said Meg.

'I have enough electricity at work. And those harsh lights. I keep a wind-up torch, batteries and a generator for emergencies.'

'Great. What a place, Colin. How did you find this? Suburgatory it is not.'

'I built it.'

'Built it? By yourself?'

'From a kit. It's a mountain hut. A Bergli. I ordered it from Switzerland.'

'These flag floors aren't Swiss.'

'No. They were under the grass. All I had to do was level them. Someone must have been here before me. And there was a rock garden of sorts at one time; which is why there are those blasted rhododendrons. But I'm clearing them, bit by bit. I hate rhododendrons.'

'Why?'

'They're alien. Wrong. Evil. They shouldn't be allowed.'

'Why do you live here?'

'Why shouldn't I?'

'Fair question, dodgy answer. So why?'

'Someone has to look after the Edge. There always is someone; always has been.'

46

'How do you know?'

'He's everywhere,' said Colin. 'If you look, you see. His face. He's obvious, in the rock, once you get your eye in.'

'"He"?' said Meg.

'Always.'

'So why you?'

'It's the only way I can be sure the Edge stays,' said Colin.

'Stays where?'

'Exists.'

'Tell me,' said Meg.

'I have to be able to see the Edge from wherever I am,' said Colin; 'in order to keep it. If something isn't looked at it may go, or change, or never be.'

'Isn't that tampering with the metaphysical?' said Meg. 'The same argument used to "prove" the existence of God. "Since we know there's a sea over the mountain, someone must be observing the sea, the mountain and us. Ergo God."'

'But do we "know"?' said Colin.

'Well, if I've booked a flight to a conference in LA and when I get there the runway hasn't been built, I'm going to be pretty hacked off.'

'I never fly.'

'Come on,' said Meg. 'You can do better than that.'

'It's more subtle now we have quantum mechanics. You must be aware that matter can be in two places and in two states at the same instant, as both a particle and a wave. Yes?'

'I did get that far. Once upon a time.'

'And if we look at it, if that matter is observed, it can change. The very act of observing makes it change. It's not quite as simple as I'm expressing it; but that's why I have to guard the Edge: to keep it in balance.'

'But what about your job? The shenanigans of giving papers and traipsing round the world all the time?'

'I don't travel.'

'Ever?'

'I mustn't be away overnight.'

'How can you not be? You're an authority, probably the main authority, on your subject. I do my homework. I've read up on you. You're the tops.'

'I can write without leaving here,' said Colin. 'Someone else gives the papers.'

'But you must have to show your face.'

'Meg. You're embarrassing me.'

'How's that?'

'I don't have to show my face. There are video links. If people care enough about my work to discuss it, they come to me.'

'Here?'

'At the telescope. No one comes here. It's private.'

'So I've intruded.'

'That's all right. You weren't to know.'

'I'm sorry.'

'Now look who's apologising.'

'But what if you were taken sick?' said Meg. 'What if you had to be hospitalised, an illness, surgery?'

'I'm never ill,' said Colin. 'I must never need or have surgery. Don't talk about it!'

'I'll take a raincheck on that,' said Meg. 'It smacks of the three-card trick to me. Shall we drink this tea before it's stewed?'

'You don't understand.'

'If it's right for you, Colin, I'm happy,' said Meg. 'I try not to be dumb, but I'm out of my depth here, I'm afraid. Will you be mother, or shall I?'

'You,' said Colin. 'I may spill it. I shake when I'm upset.'

'I had noticed.'

'I'm sorry.'

'Oh, do belt up, darling,' said Meg. She poured the tea.

'Thanks.'

'How was the scan?'

'The noise was amazing,' said Colin. 'It was all around me. It sounded as though I was in a flock of birds: cranes, *Grus grus*, would you believe it? And the sky was a spinning tunnel, with stars; five-pointed; red. Oh, and I heard her voice. She told me she was here.'

'Did she, forsooth? And you weren't bothered?'

'I know she's here now. She's close. She's staying.'

'The results came through yesterday,' said Meg. 'Where's your computer? It's not driven by elastic, or water-powered, is it?'

'Help yourself,' said Colin. 'But please keep it clear of the tea.'

'I shall. I shall, bossy boots; never you fret.'

Meg took a memory stick out of her pocket and plugged it in. 'I want you to look at this.' Colin moved a chair to sit beside her. The screen showed an array of images.

'So that's me,' said Colin. 'All that I am.'

'Perhaps,' said Meg. 'They've gone through your brain in slices.'

'And?'

'Everything's fine.' She selected a consecutive sequence and made it one whole. 'Except for this.'

'I can't read it,' said Colin. 'You'll have to talk me through.'

'It's the area here,' said Meg. 'In the right ventral frontal cortex and white matter, including the uncinate fasciculus.'

'I'm lost,' said Colin.

Meg zoomed in. 'Well, to put it simply, this shouldn't look like that.'

'How do you mean?'

'There's trauma. Quite severe trauma. Have you ever had a head injury?'

'Not that I know of.'

'A bad car accident, or anything similar?'

'Never.'

'A fall from a height, or something fall on you?'

'No.'

'Hmm.' Meg lodged her chin in her hand and scrolled between the images. 'Hmm.' The skull and brain bobbed. 'Hmm. Colin. Have you ever been struck by lightning?'

Colin knocked the computer into Meg's lap and turned his face to the log wall.

'I'm sorry! I didn't mean it!'

'Well, have you?'

'I didn't mean it! Promise I didn't!'

She put her arm round his shoulder. 'It's all right, love. It's all right.'

'How can you tell? You weren't there! Why don't you go away? Leave me alone!'

She went outside.

'Meg, I'm—'

'Don't say "sorry".'

'But I am.'

'Oh, Colin. Cheer up. I tell you what. Show us your telescope. Come on. Just for Meg. Eh?'

'Now?'

'Why not? You'll need something to keep the wind out; and there's a helmet in the pannier. Hold the grip behind you. Come on, our kid.'

'I've got to change my trousers.'

'I'll wait for you on the track,' said Meg. She started the engine and walked astride the bike to help it over the ground. Colin caught up with her, lodged on the pillion seat and they set off down Artists Lane.

'Aren't you going a bit fast?' he shouted in her ear.

'Maybe.'

'Watch for the bend at Brynlow. This is a rat run and the road narrows there.'

'Roger.'

They reached the Cross.

'I'm taking the main road.'

'Do you know the way?' said Colin.

'Yep. Hold tight.'

Meg twisted the throttle and they moved out of riding and became a part of the road's life, leaning into the bends past The Eagle and Child and pursuing the straights, overtaking the cars with dark windows, curving round the high trucks. The wind thrummed.

'Why so fast?' His hands locked on the steel bar.

'Relaxation. Concentrates the mind. Enjoy!'

The traffic lights were in their favour at Monks' Heath. The loneliness of Sodger's Hump with its ring of pines zipped by; Capesthorne and the double bend dark with rhododendron, out onto the clear ridge with the length of Redesmere on the left, the glittering water and the scudding bright sheets of the sailing club's yachts.

'Who-whoop! Wo-whoop! Wo-o-o-o! Cowabunga!'

Then to Siddington, to the salt road; wood and valley and stream swept by, field and hedge and lane; by Windyharbour, Welltrough, Withington.

'Meg! Slow down! I don't like it! Please!'

'That's because you're not the one in control!'

The telescope sprang up and dominated the land. Meg eased the throttle. The hedges became bushes and fencing again, with trees. The telescope grew. Meg crossed the road to the staff entrance. Colin unlocked the gate.

'Switch off your phone,' he said. 'We're in the radio silence zone now.'

'Never use it,' said Meg. 'Can't be arsed.'

Colin locked the gate and they went on to the main complex. He punched in the door code and led the way to the control room.

'Hello, Owen.'

'Hi, Colin.'

'I've a visitor, a friend. Is it all right to come in?'

'Be my guests.'

Beyond the round table the window framed the telescope. On either side were monitor screens and the clocks of other time.

'Meg, this is Owen. He drives the telescope.'

'Hi, Owen.'

'Hi, Meg.'

Meg looked about her. 'Wow. How do you live with it?'

'Oh, she's only a scrap-metal rustbucket and a bit of old wire,' said Owen. 'And there's never much on the telly.'

'Mm,' said Meg.

'What's today?' said Colin.

'Ethel,' said Owen.

'Mind if we have a snoop around? Is it OK to go downstairs?'

'Feel free. There may be a few postdocs to trip over.'

'And is Gwen still here?'

'No. You'll be all right. Titselina Bumsquirt went home as soon as she shut the shop.'

'Thanks, Owen,' said Colin.

'Yes. Thank you very much,' said Meg. 'It's a privilege to see this.'

'You're welcome,' said Owen.

They left the control room down a flight of stairs.

'Ethel?' said Meg.

'When you work here you have to make it family, or you wouldn't cope,' said Colin. 'Ethel's a quasar so far away that the signal started out before our galaxy was fully formed.'

'Do you always use female names? Owen called the telescope "she".'

'I suppose we do. I hadn't noticed.'

'Like anything else you can't handle. Think about it.'

They came to a room that was a clutter of cables, looped, coiled, held with plastic ties and lengths of string; lights twinkling; the chatter of printers.

'What's this gubbins here?' said Meg.

'The main control for all the telescopes linked to us on the network,' said Colin.

'But some of it seems like it's made of bits of Meccano. Why aren't you more high-tech?'

'There isn't always the equipment,' said Colin. 'We codge as we go along. It works. Which is all that matters.'

'Great. This is what I call science. This is real.'

'Come and see this, then.' He led her to a printer. Pens were moving up and down, tracing lines on graph paper. 'Behold our Ethel. The energy that's moving those pens has been travelling at two hundred and ninety-nine thousand seven hundred and ninety-one point eight one nine zero zero eight kilometres a second, approximately, for over twelve billion years, and the antenna of the telescope has picked it up and fed it down when we happen to arrive together from our separate existences and our origins in other stars to observe it here.'

'The impossibility of "now". Discuss,' said Meg.

'Follow me,' said Colin.

They went on, to a bare concrete corridor fitted with bulkhead lights, the floor wet red mud, cement stalactites hanging from the gaps in the roof slabs, up more steps, and were out in the open, among girders.

'Where's the telescope?' said Meg.

'Look up.'

'Heligoland, Dogger and Forties.'

They were at the central spot. Above them, tilted to follow Ethel, the telescope filled the sky.

'Listen,' said Colin.

Around them the wind played the harp of the structure. As the telescope moved on its track with the Earth's turn, the changes of stress made their symphony from the flexing of the metal.

'Good, isn't it?'

'Colin, this is one of the most moments,' said Meg.

'"Rustbucket scrap and a bit of old wire."'

'Hoh yes,' said Meg. 'Thank you. You don't know how much. I'm beginning to see.'

'My pleasure,' said Colin.

He went to the security fence and unlocked the gate.

'And here are the dishes.'

'Wait on,' said Meg. 'I've got to adjust.' She looked back at the telescope. 'OK. What's next?'

The parabolic dishes were nothing after the sky.

'This is where she spoke,' said Colin. 'I'm afraid I'm wobbly.'

'Let's sit down,' said Meg. She breathed out. And in. 'Right. And you understand and can handle all that up there: what it is, what it means, what it implies?'

'More or less,' said Colin. 'As well as any.'

'But not these tins.'

'Everything's relative. What do you make of them?'

'Shall we find out?'

They went to a dish. 'You understand the principle?' said Colin.

'Near enough. Do I go to the other end?'

'Keep your voice low,' said Colin. 'Whisper. And stay at the focus.'

Meg went.

'Hi, Colin. How's that?'

'Spot on.'

'Weird, isn't it?'

'And if someone stood in the acoustic line between they'd hear both of us, but the sound would have no direction,' said Colin.

'Would it internalise?' said Meg.

'More ambient, though unnatural in space.'

'Like another dimension?'

'I suppose it would be.'

'What are you going to do with the dishes you're making?'

'Fiddle around with them. Listen.'

'Listen to what?'

'Whatever the dishes may reflect.'

'Whatever?'

'Yes. That's the way to do it.'

'Hello, Col.'

'It's not funny, Meg.'

'What isn't?'

'Stop it.'

'Stop what?'

'She can't hear me, Col.'

'Is it you? Is it?'

'Of course.'

'Please. Stay.'

'I'm not going anywhere. Don't turn round. You know what happens when men look back.'

'The years. The searching.'

'Colin. This is Meg. Are you all right?'

'Go away, Meg.'

'I'm still here, Col. She'll try to be rid of me. She wants me gone. But she'll have no luck. Don't you know who she is? Don't you remember?'

'What? Remember what?'

'It's her, Col. She's come to get you. This time.'

'No.'

'Yes. But I'll stop her.'

'Where are you?'

'With you, Col. I'm always with you.'

'Where? Why can't I see you?'

'Ah.'

'I must see you.'

'Why?'

'You're my pearl.'

'Yes, I'm your pearl.'

'My pearl to a white pea.'

'That's a funny thing to say.'

'But you are. Let me across.'

'Colin. Meg here. Look round. Look at me. Look now. I'm telling you. Now.'

'She's hurting, Col. She's hurting me. It hurts. Don't let her. It hurts. Don't look. It hurts. Col. The others. They're coming.'

His head was blistered in noise, swamped by calling, around him, in him. He fell into the sound of cranes.

Colin hit the asphalt at the bottom of the steps and lay. He looked back. Meg was at the other dish, turned towards him. She came down and stood over him.

'You're only winded.'

He grabbed for air.

'Now what was all that about?' said Meg.

'I've found her. She spoke.'

'I bet she did. Let's check, then. Sailor's grip.' Meg gave a lift to Colin and he pulled himself up to sit on a step. Meg sat by him, holding a recorder. She pressed the playback.

'What are you going to do with the dishes you're making? Fiddle around with them. Listen. Listen to what? Whatever the dishes may reflect. Whatever? Yes. That's the way to do it. It's not funny, Meg. What isn't? Stop it. Stop what? Is it you? Is it? Please. Stay. The years. The searching. Colin. This is Meg. Are you all right? Go away, Meg. What? Remember what? No. Where are you? Where? Why can't I see you? I must see you. You're my pearl. My pearl to a white pea. But you are. Let me across. Colin. Meg here. Look round. Look at me. Look now. I'm telling you. Now.'

'That's all.' Meg switched off.

Colin put his hand out and she took it.

'Oh, my God.'

Meg was silent.

56

'My God.'

His grip crushed, but she did not flinch.

'I am mad. I am mad. Aren't I?'

'You are not mad,' she said. 'Yet.'

'I heard her.'

'Of course you heard her. What did she say?'

'She's with me. Always. Always will be. She doesn't like you. Says you've come to get me. She'll stop you. What am I going to do?'

'Don't panic. You'll live. But you're not fit to be on a bike. Sit quiet. We'll see you home.'

He held Meg's hand; she looked at the telescope. It tracked the quasar, and the wind played.

'Come up, love.'

He walked with her; he still held; out past the car park. There was a car waiting.

'Now then, our Colin,' said Bert. 'Are you all right? Let's be having you.'

Then he came to the age where he could not run. Pain sat in his knee, so that he stumbled, and in his arm, so that his spear did not hit. Pain sat in his back, so that he could not lift the kill and fetch it home, nor bring wood from far, so that his fire was small. He preyed upon the weak and gained no strength. He took the deer big-bellied, ripped out the fawn, leaving the hind to crows. Wolf and raven followed him. He took the farrow and fled the sow; until there was only fox to hunt. He ate nothing that drew its spirit from the cave, and his own spirit dwindled unfed. He set traps for hare.

He knew how this had been before, and the old man had fetched meat that had no song. But the old man had taught him to hunt and kill, so that he came to know the way of the beasts, and after he had taken the old man to the nooks of the dead he had stayed. The old man had taught him to free the

57

spirits from the rock, to dance and sing and dream. Now there was no one to be taught. And no woman came.

'I found my love in the month of June.
Risselty-rosselty, now, now, now.
I carried her home in a silver spoon.
Risselty-rosselty, hey bombossity,
Knickerty-knackerty,
Now, now, now.'
At the quarry, Colin adjusted his dishes on their mountings.
'I lost my love in the dark of the moon.
Risselty-rosselty, now, now, now.
If she came back it would not be soon.
Risselty-rosselty, hey donny-dossity,
Knickerty-knackerty, rustical quality,
Willow tree wallowty
Now, now, now.'
He attached the focus rings.
'There's bread and cheese upon the shelf,
Risselty-rosselty, now, now, now.
If you want any more you can sing it yourself.
Risselty-rosselty, hey bombossity,
Knickerty-knackerty, rustical quality,
Willow tree wallowty, hey donny-dossity,
Risselty-rosselty
Now, now, now.'
Colin brought a chair and sat facing in. He put his mouth at the focus. 'Hello, I'm here. Hello. Hello.'

It hurt to turn the stick between his palms to blow a fire heap. It hurt to follow his shoulder and to twist his head through the hill along the seam of grit. It hurt to cut the veil to set the spirits free. His hand on the blade lost its grace, and it hurt to make a beast true. Yet if he did not make it true the spirit would not be true. Beasts would go into the world unmade. Wolves would feed until there were no more, and then wolves and all would pass because they had eaten life rough-hewn. The Stone Spirit and the Bull would see that the land was wrong and dead, and there would be no eagles sent to feed the stars; the sun would not turn from death, and there would be only wanderers and the moon and Crane flying in night.

There had to be a woman that he could hold, to grow a child that he could teach, to stop the dark. But where she was he could not dream.

He climbed down into the great cave, beneath the bulls and above the shining waters, seeing nothing outside the glimmer in which he hung. He came to the Stone and sat a while, moving his thought. Then he danced and sang. He became the sounds, and was with the voices of the old, and the voices of the old were with him. His step crushed, and under him rose light, which lifted into him and flowed from bone to bone along his spine and every rib, gleamed at his fingers, filled his skull, broke through his eyes, and brought pictures to his tongue.

The light threw a shaft across the wall, and he saw a way he did not know. He followed, turning to fit the crack. The waters were near. He stretched. He touched a nipple, hard in the rock.

Colin pressed the bell.

Meg opened the door. 'Hello, stranger. Come in.' She led the way to the library and curled up on the chaise longue. Colin stood by the window, looking towards Beeston. 'I got your letter,' she said.

'I hope it didn't cause offence,' said Colin.

'Was it meant to?'

'No. I wanted to thank you.'

'For what?'

'Taking me seriously. And to say that I don't need to waste any more of your time.'

59

'So why are you here?'

'Because you're kind—'

'Bullshit.'

'—and a letter isn't the right way to say goodbye.'

'I don't say goodbye.'

'There's nothing wrong now,' said Colin. 'I was a mess, and you sorted me out. I'm going back to work. As soon as I've seen my doctor.'

'I can't sort anyone out, dear heart,' said Meg. 'But so long as you're happy that's all that counts.' She picked up a magazine and opened it. 'Have a nice day.'

'Yes.' Colin went to the door. 'Meg. Thanks.'

'You're welcome.'

He turned the handle.

'Colin?'

'Yes?'

'One thing.'

'Yes.'

'Why did you smash the glass?'

Crow. Crane. Stone. Bone. Moon. Mother. Made. Blade. Bull. Blood.

'Witch!'

'Shush, laddie. No need to capslock. You're all right.' He sank in the deep leather and she held his hand. 'What are you so scared of?'

'You.'

'That makes sense,' said Meg.

He had found the woman. She was pressing to be brought. He had to free her spirit so that it could go into the world and come to him. If he cut wrong, she would not be whole, and no child could be made. The blade had to be pure, with no stain, so that it would lift the weight of the moon at its full.

He climbed back and took all the stone that he held in

Ludcruck: stone that he had gathered from the torrent beds, stone that the old man had brought when young, and stone from before him; the black stone and the white. He had gone with the old man up to where the Mother lay, and they had sung and danced before her, and the old man had told the stories of the Beginning, so that the Mother would let them take her bone from the land for the getting of life.

But all this had been before, and he saw that the stones too were old now and might not hear the songs that he must sing and the stories that he must tell for the stones to learn the shaping of his hand. If he cut with a blade from tired stone the woman would be tired and her belly dry, without blood.

He had heard the stories of the Beginning and the songs and the steps of the dance; and he knew the way. He had to go to the Mother while his legs could walk and dance, to bring the stone that had the life to make the blade to cut the rock to free the woman to make the child to learn the dance to keep the world. If he did not, there would be no other.

He took a fire stick and went from Ludcruck to where the sun rose at its longest.

He walked for one day, he walked for two days, he walked for three days into the further land. But he did not come to where the Mother lay. He walked past torrent beds, which led him by the cobbles of her rolled bones. He walked for four days. He walked for seven. He walked for nine. And he came to the Mother.

Her flanks were covered with scrub. He went to where he had come with the old man; but the marks of their taking had grown dead. No blades lay in that stone.

He sang and danced and told the stories of the Beginning; and he sat and dreamed. Then he took a piece of her weathered skin, and drove it, smashing away the dead flesh, maggot-cleansing the Mother, for three days till he came to the white bone. He saw the living blades within, the blades that she had

61

grown in the Beginning, the life that came from the start of things, and he sang to the Mother that the bone should not break, telling the stories as he worked, so she would know that he sang true.

The bone came free. It was as much as he could bear.

He sang to the Mother, to make her sleep and feel no hurt. He gathered the splinters of his work from the taking and buried them by her ribs. He lifted the bone upon his shoulder and set out under the weight. His shoulder tore, but he went on. His arms were numb; his hands did not hold. Sweat and thirst made his mind a cloud, and blood came from his eyes, but he followed the torrent beds down, and in a time he could not tell he came to the Bearstone above Ludcruck, and dropped into the cleft.

'Why am I scared of you?' said Colin.

'God knows,' said Meg. 'Do you?'

'Now I've found her everything should be right again.'

'"Again"? When was that?'

'Before I lost her.'

'Remind me. Who is "her"?'

'You don't need reminding,' said Colin. 'You mean repeat. What you don't know is she's my twin. She tells me.'

'Ah now. Twin. What's her name?'

'I can't access the data. She went before—'

'Before you were thirteen?'

'But she's real. She is. She is real.'

'What did your parents say?' said Meg.

'I can't access them.'

'Why not?'

Colin shook his head. 'They were deleted.'

'Your parents were killed. Air crash.'

'Sierra Papa Lima Tango Foxtrot.'

'I wouldn't know about that. But you were twelve years old.'

'Flight one-six-five. Was I?'

'Yes. What do you remember of your adolescence?'

'School. Holidays. University.'

'Who paid for it all?'

'I don't know.'

'Aren't you interested, Colin?'

'What happened to my sister?'

'Colin. I've tracked the records. Has it never occurred to you to do the same?'

'No.'

'You have no surviving family.'

'There's my sister. I lost her. My sister. I've been looking; searching; for years; even in the stars.'

'Where did you spend those holidays?'

'Here, on the Edge. Down Hocker Lane.'

'Who did you stay with?'

'An old man. And his wife. They were small farmers.'

'How did you come to be there?' said Meg.

'I loved them.'

'Then what?'

'He died. And she died six years after I'd got my doctorate and was at the telescope, and the farm had to be sold. It was tarted up and gentrified, and I went to Church Quarry and built the Bergli. I don't go down Hocker Lane. It's too dreadful.'

'Where were you when the amnesia began?'

'It must have been at the farm.'

'And your sister? Where was she?'

'I don't know.'

'Do you remember her being at the farm?'

'Sometimes. I can't be sure. Bits.'

'According to the records, Elizabeth Mossock, of Hocker Lane, was your legal guardian, and the couple adopted you when you were twelve. Did they ever mention a sister?'

'No,' said Colin. 'But I used to ask them.'

'And what did they say?'

'Nothing. Every time I asked they changed the subject. It seemed to upset them, though they tried not to show it. They wouldn't talk about her.'

'I'm not surprised,' said Meg.

'But they must have known, mustn't they? They could have told me. They could have said.'

'Oh, supple your kidneys. Let's not add paranoia, Colin. Now. Listen. Hear me. I'm not asking you to accept this; only to consider it. What you've been describing is well recorded in the literature. It's known as Missing Twin Syndrome. It creates the illusion of another self. It can be pathological, but it often has a physical reality, where one embryo has absorbed the other, or aborted it. Does that possibility ring any bells for you?'

'Cuckoo,' said Colin. '*Cuculus canorus*, long-tailed, rather sharp-winged; in flight sometimes confused with sparrowhawk, *Accipiter nisus*, or even kestrel, *Falco tinnunculus*, commonly windhover.'

'You are not a bird,' said Meg.

'Then where's my twin?' said Colin. 'Where's my sister? Give her back. Where is she?'

'Good question.'

'Don't ditch me, Meg.'

'I shan't.'

'What am I going to do?'

'It's a poser,' said Meg. 'Now you're presenting juvenile psychopathy. That's greedy. But getting you sectioned isn't an option. Yet. So how's about inviting me to dinner? A girl needs a break sometimes.'

'I'd like that very much,' said Colin.

'You're on,' said Meg.

When his legs could walk and his hands could hold and his fingers speak he went from the lodge the length of three days' hunting down beside the river towards the Flatlands, to the earth where the hammers grew.

He searched about the bank until he found two that were firm. One was white and black, the other yellow and grey. He pulled them from the mud and moved them in his hand. They were ripe to be taught their ways.

The hammer rocks were as hard as the Motherbone, but not so hard that they bruised or flawed the blow. They were not as fine as the bone, but glittered packed night, and stars that would fly as they hit and worked. He took them and climbed back to the hills.

He rested, shaping his thought; and the next day he went and sat in Ludcruck between the walls of making. In each hand he held a hammer stone and sang to them the story of the world and how they came to be. He told them their names and how the spirits had grown them in the earth. He told them the Motherbone that they must strike without wound and how his hand would help and his fingers teach. He moved them to find how they would turn, and to make them know how they would sit and take knowledge from his palm. He moved them so that his fingers knew to guide, and he sang for learning from the old, for them to give his eye their skill, to hit with wisdom and to guide his song. This was the last bone that he could carry from the Mother. If the blades he brought from it should break or he not cut, the woman would be kept in Ludcruck at the rock veil and the world would end.

When he had told and done he set the hammers down and fetched the Motherbone. He laid it by them and sat through the night, and he and all were singing in one dream.

At dawn he drank and fed and shat. He breathed in and a little out and breathed and breathed again. He felt the spirits wake. He took the hammer that was white and black and with it tapped the bone. He took the yellow and grey. He tapped. The one knew the way to the blades, and the other how to free them.

65

His palm held, his fingers told, his eye grew strong, his hand lifted, the spirits came, and all cried down upon the bone. It sang hurt and joy. It sang birth and making.

The hand lifted and bore again. Hammer and hand and eye and bone spoke, and the maker spirits in the walls answered and shaped their spirit blades of spirit bone. He was of them and they of him and Ludcruck rang.

On through the day he hit, and the blades rose towards him from the marrow. He rested, drank, and hit again. But though his eye was strong, his hand began to lose its thought. His fingers slurred. The voice of the bone was dulled, the hammer deaf; the spirits paused and watched. He lifted, havered, struck. The bone shattered and the blades were gone.

Pain sat all in him. His eye told his hand, but his hand did not hear. He went to the lodge, and it was cold.

He woke and felt to know that he was dead. His groin was warm. He touched his eyes. It was day. He rolled onto his knees, pushed and stood against the pain, holding the pole of the lodge. He went out to Ludcruck.

The hammers glinted, but the shards of the Mother lay spent. He gathered them and searched their veins. He saw that they were old and he had chosen wrong. Brown lines of blood that could not live again ran deep. His eye had not heard. The world was lost through him.

He turned the last piece. It was no bigger than two hands. The brown ran through all the weight that he had brought; but ended here. In this one fist there was no flaw. He took the white and black, and tapped. The bone answered, and it was another song, deep where he could not see. He took the yellow and grey. He tapped. He took the white and black again and worked down into the bone. He stopped and tapped with yellow and grey.

He went on, unfettering the rock. Something lay within. It was close, though he could not see. He came upon it as he would a hare. Tak. Tak. Tak. Tak. Tak.

At his most gentle touch the bone split and stole the dawn. He covered his face and looked between his fingers. In the last hope of the Mother lay a rod of light. Its ridges were crests of blades worked by other hands, hands from the Beginning, waiting in the bone. He lifted it. The Mother had given. The spirits laughed.

He took the blades and trimmed their crests, strengthened their edges with pressing and soft blows. He went down into Ludcruck, his mind hard against pain, past the nooks of the dead, along the seam of grit, by the clamour of beasts, down the cliff to the great cave and the Stone above the shining waters. He sat by the Stone, moving his thought, and then he danced until the moon lifted in him, brought pictures to his tongue and shone across the wall to the gap. He followed, twisting at the crack. The waters were near. He stretched. He touched the nipple in the rock.

He shifted back and raised his lamp. The swelling of the veil was more than he could pass as the woman pushed, but there was a groove beneath. He lay flat and crawled under the belly, though he could scarcely go. His arm, head and shoulder led him through, and the lamp showed the space beyond.

He stood, and looked back. Now he saw the breast. From here he could cut the veil. He set the lamp where it would light the work, and he took a blade and put it to the rock where the nipple thrust. And then he cut, guiding his hand with song.

He carved the breast, and when it was clear he followed the throat to open the mouth so that the woman could breathe. He marked the eyes so that they might see the way, and shaped the head so that it would turn. Then he worked the other breast for milk to flow.

He curved the belly full of life and cut the slot wide to bring the birth. He shaped one arm to hold to the breasts, another to hold the young moon, and legs to stand and to be cranes to fly to carry the spirit across the land.

And when that was done he rested and lay deep in Ludcruck by the waters until he had the strength to climb, back from the cave, by the clamour of the beasts, along the seam of grit, past the nooks of the dead, into the day and the loud crag.

The woman was free; and she would come to him.

'Hi,' said Meg. 'Am I too early?'

'No. No. Not at all,' said Colin. 'How did you get here?'

'Bert dropped me off. I hoped we might go for a walk.'

'Of course,' said Colin.

'I'd like you to show me the Edge.'

'That could last for ever,' said Colin. 'But we can take a stroll, if you like.'

'Strolling is what I do best.'

'Splendid. I'll just pop the lamb in the oven. Oh, thoughtless of me. I didn't ask. Are you vegetarian?'

'Carnivore,' said Meg. 'And I like my lamb pink.'

'Good.' He unhooked his plain gown from behind the door and put it on. 'Allow me.'

They left the quarry and walked through the woods.

'Of course,' said Colin, 'you have to bear in mind that all this is eighteenth-century landscaping. Before, it was called a "dreary common".'

'Well, it isn't now,' said Meg. 'Hush.'

'Sor—'

'Ah?'

'—ry.'

They walked without speaking. Colin led the way down into a deep hollow. The floor was uneven and they skirted mud. The sides were cut straight, herringbone patterned by picks. It was another old quarry, huge and grassy. At the end Meg stopped. Pines stood above on the rim, and their roots had teased down and split the rock with life. The stone was pure, without blemish or grain, but near the bottom of the wall was a bed of red marl. The clay had weathered out, leaving a shelf. Meg reached up and took some in her hand and worked it on her palm, spitting to make it soft. Then she lifted her finger and drew it across Colin's forehead and on his cheekbones and along his nose. He could not see what she was doing, but the marks were careful and even, matching either side. Her brow was furrowed, her finger light, precise. She looked, smiled and put her arm through his as they went out of the quarry, by a cut gap along a path, with a cleft on each side, to a broad way, and ahead was treeless sky.

'Wow. What's this? Where are we?' said Meg.

'Stormy Point.'

The ground was sand and quartz pebbles: loose pebbles lying and pebbles in the rock. Stone thrust out. Below, the scarp was tumbled with boulders to the land beneath. The brindled fields stretched to the hills. Meg sat on a rock to see, but Colin shook his head.

'Not here. Not now. Keep moving.'

'Why?' said Meg.

'There are things to show you, and I don't want to overcook the lamb.'

'That path's interesting.'

'No. This way. Another time, perhaps.'

'But where does it go?'

'Saddlebole. Too far.'

'And what's Saddlebole?'

'A spur, that's all.'

They were back among trees. The scarp curved in a horseshoe. The path had been rerouted, but Colin took her down along an older one, with the wall on their left and the drop to their right.

'What the flipping heck is this?' said Meg.

They were below a pointed wedge of the hill that jutted high above the path.

'Castle Rock,' said Colin. 'It's the most instructive part of the Edge. It shows the Permo-Triassic boundary clearly. Which is why it's so remarkable. Here, where we are, the polychromatic sandstone has eroded because it's a soft aeolian desert and the grains have lost their facets through being worked by the wind; hence all the graffiti. Then above, a slow estuarine feature has moved in, hard, with no inclusions. And above it is the conglomerate, without stratification but full of derived quartz pebbles, indicating high-energy flow, a torrential fluvial deposit.'

'It's the colours that get me,' said Meg. 'They're psychedelic almost.'

'Come this way.' He led her around a corner to the further side. 'Look at this.' A streak of green showed under lichen. 'Malachite. Hydrated copper carbonate. The Edge is full of it, in a manner of speaking. But here is its furthest exposure in this direction. Now look across to the left and up a bit. Can you see anything?'

'No.'

'Try again.'

'Well, I'll go to Leek and Ludchurch!'

'What do you see?'

'It's a carving.'

'Of what?'

'I don't know. It's so weathered. Concentric squares? It's not a face. Is it? Or is it? Not squares? More trapezoidal? A labyrinth? Maybe.'

'Must it be "either or"?' said Colin.

'You mean a doodle?' said Meg.

'A doodle is meaningless, random. This isn't random, what-ever else it is. And it's taken skill and effort and time. There's no way that that can be a doodle; and I don't think it was done with metal, either.'

'So what is it? What's it for?'

'I've no idea. A territorial marker? Perhaps a claim. A warning.

70

An indication of a special place? Whatever it is it signifies something important about here, or even another dimensional boundary. Or all. Or more.'

'If I were playing hard to get,' said Meg, 'I'd say that you were claiming it's whatever you want to see. It's a Rorschach blot.'

'That's your modern thought,' said Colin. 'We have to make the imaginative leap into the ancient mind and the likelihood of a different world view. I agree that you could argue that for a thing to have a multitude of possible meanings is tantamount to its having no meaning at all. But perhaps the opposite could once have applied. Perhaps a thing that could be thought to have a multitude of meaning, then, gained strength and importance from the ambiguities. We simply don't know. Nor is there any way of our knowing, at the present, whatever "the present" may be; but we must keep our minds open; though, yes, not so open that our brains drop out.'

'OK,' said Meg. 'It's old. But how old is old?'

'It looks Neolithic or Bronze Age,' said Colin, 'but I'd say possibly Mesolithic, if Mesolithic is possible; which it may not be.'

'Why Mesolithic?'

'I'm best-guessing. Look there. That overhang further along is perfect for a rock shelter.'

'But we've seen plenty like that.'

'But not like this one.'

A path with steps came between Castle Rock and the overhang. Colin went to it and bent down, scanning the ground.

'Here we are.' He picked something up and went on looking. 'And another. And another. That last lot of rain we had was useful. And another. Another.'

He held out his palm. On it lay five splinters of pale stone.

'And?' said Meg.

'Microliths. Flint. Flint doesn't occur here naturally; it has

71

to have been imported. Someone brought it, and sat by Castle Rock and knapped it. These are diagnostic Mesolithic, eight to ten thousand years ago. They've been waiting for us to handle them and recognise what they are for the first time since the end of the last Ice Age. We may even share DNA with the person that made them.' He threw the flints back to the land.

'Why don't you keep them?'

'That would compromise the site. Shall we see how the lamb's doing? It'll be about right by now, I should think, wouldn't you?'

'You're a strange one,' said Meg. 'Sometimes you are very strange. "Compromise".'

They climbed round and to the top of Castle Rock.

The ancient river bed had been quarried into planes and low benches of ledge, and the prow of the rock smooth, drawing up to the point where it stood over air.

'This is terrific,' said Meg.

'Careful,' said Colin. 'You need a head for heights here.'

'That's what I've got,' said Meg.

'Well, I haven't,' said Colin. 'This is as far as I can go.' He sat on one of the ledges, away from the drop.

Meg went to the tip of the point and looked down and about her. 'Wow.' She spread her arms. 'Wow! Whee!'

'Please,' said Colin.

'What a view,' said Meg. 'And the wind's great. I could fly.'

'Don't,' said Colin.

'Geronimo!'

'Please come back, Meg.'

She began to whistle a tune.

'What's that?' he said.

'Something we used to sing in the playground at school.'

'I've heard it before.'

'I shouldn't wonder. You were a kid once. We all were.'

'Please come away from there,' said Colin. 'You're making my insteps hurt.'

Meg turned round, her back to the drop. 'It can't harm you,' she said. 'The rock has no opinion.'

'Hasn't it? Please.'

'You great mardy. You're frit.' But she came and sat by him and looked to the hills. She hummed the tune.

'What is that?' said Colin.

'You know,' she said, and began to sing quietly and slowly.

'The wind, the wind, the wind blows high.

The rain comes pattering down the sky.

She is handsome, she is pretty,

She is the girl of the windy city.

She has lovers, one, two, three;

Pray will you tell me who is she?'

'I know it. Somewhere,' said Colin. 'Yes. Bert whistled it. But I have heard it before, too.'

'I tell you what,' said Meg. 'I'm ready for that lamb.'

'Of course,' said Colin.

'Come on then. Let's go. Doesn't the telescope look good from here?' Away to the south the structure stood out from the land as a bowl, pointing straight up. 'What's it doing?'

'Nothing at the moment,' said Colin. 'It's in the zenith; what we call "parked".'

'At this distance it's a goblet, or even a chalice. It could be the Grail.'

'It's certainly a Questing tool,' said Colin.

They left Castle Rock by a shorter way and came to Church Quarry from the side and down a path to the hut. Colin hung up his gown and opened the oven door.

'Mm. Smells delicious,' said Meg.

Colin tried the meat with a fork. 'Perfect.' He lifted it out and set it to stand.

The table was already laid.

'I like your silver,' said Meg.

'It needs to be used.'

'Couldn't agree more. If you've got it, flaunt it, that's my motto.'

Colin put an oil lamp on the table. He lifted off the globe of frosted glass, and removed the clear chimney. He set them side by side and took a pair of scissors and trimmed the two wicks, lit them, and turned them down until they burned a low flame. He left it for a while, then he fitted the chimney back on.

'What I can't stomach about period films,' he said, 'is that no one knows how to light a lamp. They're always flaring and smoking and the top of the chimney's black with soot. It kills all credibility. You have to start cool, wait for the glass to warm, and turn the wick up gently to give a clear flame. Like—' He checked that the wicks were level, and lowered the globe over the chimney. '—so.' He chose wood to put on the fire.

'You can't beat a log fire, can you?' said Meg. 'It's atavistic.'

'And it warms you three times,' said Colin. 'Once fetching, once splitting, once burning. But you have to know how to use that over there.'

'Hey. Some axe.'

'Scandinavian. They're the best. But you can't fool around with them. If you do, you're dead.'

'It must be four foot, if it's an inch.' Meg went to the corner where the axe stood and put her finger to the edge. 'Sharp as a razor. I see you keep it greased.'

'If you let it get dull the energy is dissipated through friction,' said Colin. 'And if rust takes hold you might as well thump wedges. Here's another lost art.' He took sheets of newspaper and rolled each tightly across from corner to corner to make a thin rod. He bent the rod into a triangle, leaving the two ends long so that he could turn them back and weave and lock them between the three sides. Then he crumpled a sheet loosely in the grate and laid the triangles on the paper. He built grids of

74

kindling on top at right angles to each other. 'The secret is to make plenty of room for air.'

'Where did you learn all that palaver with rolling the paper?' said Meg.

'At the farm, I imagine.' Colin chose small logs, arranged them above and around the kindling, and lit the loose paper. 'The rule is, "One log can't burn. Two logs won't burn. Three logs make a fire." And mix them. Ash, thorn and oak are best, if it's heat you want. Birch, holly and fir for brightness.'

The rolled sheets were red, and blue flame spurted from their ends. The kindling caught.

'Brilliant,' said Meg. 'Strange how things often come in threes, isn't it?'

'Simple physics, in this case.'

'But who worked out the trinities? Ash, thorn, oak. Birch, holly, fir. Timber. Logs. Firelighters.'

'Empirical pragmatism,' said Colin. 'Nothing mystical or esoteric; though some would have it so. Now let's have a whiff of adventure, shall we?' He fitted a head torch on his brow and opened the door.

The hut sat in a corner of the quarry, and at the junction of the two sides was a tunnel into the rock. It had a gate of iron bars. He unlocked the gate and pushed it open.

'I want to show you something special. I think there'll be enough daylight. There it is. Look along the wall near the floor to the right. What can you see?'

'Rock,' said Meg.

'What's on the rock, just at the edge of darkness?'

'Oh, yes! It's beautiful! The rock's glowing. Green. Green jewels.'

'Go and touch them.'

Meg went into the tunnel.

'They've scarpered! There's nothing here!'

'Come back to the entrance and look again,' said Colin.

'Yes! I can see them! What is it?'

'Goblin gold,' said Colin. 'More correctly, *Schistostega pennata*. It's a moss; quite rare. It grows at the limit of photo-synthesis, where there's no competition. The effect's caused by the protonemata, which have adapted to capture the light in a narrow focus; a bit like cats' eyes on a road. So when you're at the right distance and angle they reflect. But when you go up close they appear to vanish; hence the popular name.'

'You're a rum little devil, our Colin,' said Meg.

'Party tricks. I don't really "know" very much, if anything, at all.'

'Well, you know more than me.'

'Don't we all tend to dismiss our own areas of expertise?'

Meg looked at him. 'Now that's insight. Though I still don't see why an astrophysicist needs to know about moss. You're daft, but you're not stupid.'

'The electro-magnetic spectrum is what's in common,' said Colin. 'Now let's get ourselves something to complement the meal.'

He stepped up into the tunnel and switched on his torch.

'What is this?' said Meg.

'Questions, always questions,' said Colin. 'It's a trial adit to test the quality of the rock. It runs along the horizon between the conglomerate and the dimension stone.'

'So the next question is: what's dimension stone?'

Colin laughed. 'Now that is a very good question. Which is it? Eighth? Ninth? Eleventh? Twelfth? Nth? Who can tell? But it's only the term the quarrymen used for the fine unlaminated sandstones that cut well in all directions. They drove the adit to see whether it was worth extending the quarry. It wasn't; so they stopped after twenty-seven metres. But it still has its worth. It makes an excellent cellar. Come along.'

'The way the pebbles catch the light,' said Meg. 'They're big, too.'

'Yes; and fine specimens. But we need to be further in, where it's darker.'

The entrance to the adit was round and wide, and became a narrower slot where Colin had to stoop.

'Here should be about right.' Colin took two small quartz pebbles from his pocket and switched off the torch. 'Watch this.' He held one in each hand and rubbed them hard together.

'Oh!'

There was a shimmer of cold moonlight from the pebbles.

'That's beautiful!' said Meg.

Colin rubbed them again. Again the light. He lifted a hand to the roof and rubbed one of the big pebbles in the rock. The light was brighter.

'How do you do it?'

'Triboluminescence,' said Colin. 'To oversimplify. Quartz, and bone for that matter, is a substance that contains piezo-electrical charge which changes polarisation when mechanical stress is applied, which manifests itself as light. We don't know for sure how this happens, but one theory is that the impact causes electrons to jump to a higher energy shell, then when they jump back to the original shell orbit their transition creates the light.'

'Yes, I did ask, didn't I?' said Meg. 'I did ask. I did. Wae's me. I did.'

'Quartz is the second most abundant mineral in the Earth's crust, and is made up of a framework of silicon-oxygen tetrahydra,' said Colin. 'And silicon lies directly below carbon in the periodic table, so that much of its basic chemistry is similar to carbon, which is the foundation of life here; which makes me wonder whether we're merely carbon chauvinists.'

'Breathe in,' said Meg.

'I'm not out of breath.'

'I am.'

'Theoretically,' said Colin, 'under the right conditions, you could have a silicon-based life source, and I personally am prepared to accept that, though the evidence for it is not yet stable. But, as we all know, "absence of evidence is not evidence of absence." The idea of a quartz bone appeals to me.'

'Stupid of me not to think of that,' said Meg. 'Tut.'

'Carbon, however, is more adaptive. Which is why we're more than soggy bags of electrolytes. Am I boring you, am I?'

'You are not boring me,' said Meg. 'You're more fun than living with a library. Stone bone. I like that. It sounds right.'

'Your library's far bigger,' said Colin. 'And much better looking.'

'Oh, flattery, flattery,' said Meg. 'Stone bone. Bone stone. Mm.'

'Let's see, now.' Colin switched the torch back on. 'What have we here?'

One side of the adit was lined with wine racks. Colin moved along the rows of bottles.

'I think this one,' he said. 'And this. Ah, and I hadn't thought of these. They'll do nicely.'

The adit was straight, and from the end the day showed as a nimbus of another world.

'And while we're here—'

'Colin, we can't drink this much. We'll be paralytic.'

'Choice, Meg, choice. Quality and balance. We may carouse without oblivion. There's a difference between inebriation and exultation. The god within and the god without.'

'Just so long as you can tell the difference,' said Meg.

'There's no point in drinking if you are unable to recall the taste,' said Colin. 'Here. Take these two, please. Careful. It would be a tragedy to drop them.'

They went back to the entrance and Colin locked the gate.

'New potatoes, carrots and broccoli, with garlic bread. How does that sound?'

'It sounds pretty good to me,' said Meg. 'Did you grow all this yourself?'

'Apart from the dead sheep. I'll just show the broccoli the water while we have an aperitif.' Colin opened a bottle and poured into crystal glass. 'Welcome to Imazaz, Meg.'

'Thanks, Colin. Cheers. Down the hatch. Whoa! This is the real stuff!'

'What else should it be?' said Colin.

He lay in the lodge and waited. She would come. Now she would come. He knew.

'A drop more to finish your plate?' said Colin.

'Thanks. What I'd like to know is how do you manage to keep a perspective?' said Meg. 'Don't you get lost in it all? The immensities?'

'It's only maths.'

'"Only".'

'Well of course it's difficult to begin with,' said Colin. 'You have to try not to think of the implications while you're assembling the data. My first professor had a way of dealing with that. He said that if we go out to the limit of the cosmos and in, to the sub-atomic extreme, the human body is more or less at the middle of mensuration. We're at the point of balance. It may well be that we are that point of balance. Now, since he said it, I can show, from our present knowledge of the cosmos, that he was wrong; but then I don't know how far the particle physicists have moved in the other direction. We may still be at the middle. And that's only for this universe. Anyway, it's a helpful reference point to keep in mind.'

'Leonardo would have loved your professor,' said Meg.

'But there's always the moment when the data are all collected and it's just you and them,' said Colin. 'That's when it can be hard. You're on your own. But it doesn't happen every week, thank goodness. Then you have to treat it as a game, and play around; and sooner or later you "see" the obvious; though proving it can take longer. Much longer. But, at the heart, all discovery is play.'

'How do you know when you've finished?'

'Oh, there's no finish. Sometimes you see the answer first, then spend years finding what the question is. That's the nearest you come to finishing. This is donkey and carrot country. If I ever finished, I don't know what I'd do. I might as well peel potatoes.'

'There's nothing wrong with scrubbing a few spuds,' said Meg, 'to go with the carrots; very tasty, by the way. But are you saying there's no final answer?'

'I hope there isn't,' said Colin. 'I'm for uncertainty. As soon as you think you know, you're done for. You don't listen and you can't hear. If you're certain of anything, you shut the door on the possibility of revelation, of discovery. You can think. You can believe. But you can't, you mustn't, "know". There's the real entropy.'

'How come?'

'I can show you best with a story.'

'Oh, stories! Stories freak me out. Tell me one.'

'Right,' said Colin, and took a mouthful of wine. 'Ready? Well. One day, Vishnu, otherwise Delta Capricorni, is sitting alone on the top of Chomolungma.'

'What's that?'

'The highest of all mountains.'

'Do you mean Everest?'

'That's an imposed, impertinent, imperial arrogance,' said Colin. 'Its name is Chomolungma; or Sagarmāthā. Now shall I tell you this story or not?'

'Oops. Into the Naughty Corner, Meg. Please tell me the story.'

'Right. So Vishnu is sitting on the top of Chomolungma, and crying.'

'Why?'

'Oh, Meg. Do be quiet. You're worse than a child.'

She turned her mouth down.

'Vishnu is crying. And along comes Hanuman, Alpha Boötes, the monkey god, and he says, "Why are you crying? And what are all those ants down there on the Earth so excited about?" "They're not ants," says Vishnu. "They're people. I was holding the Jewel of Absolute Wisdom; and I dropped it; and it fell into the World and broke. Everybody down there has got a tiny splinter of it; but they each think they've got the whole thing, and they're all running around and shouting and telling each other, but no one is listening." That's the story.'

'Wow. That's a true story,' said Meg. 'Just love it.'

'For "ants" you could substitute "cosmologists",' said Colin.

'And most of the medical fraternity,' said Meg. 'So there's the reason why you'd rather be the donkey.'

'There's the reason why I'd rather be the donkey.'

'I'll take a high five on that,' said Meg.

'Take a what?' said Colin.

'Never mind,' said Meg, and lowered her hand.

'Think about it,' said Colin. 'If a painter ever achieved perfection, what else would there be to do? The same goes for a sculptor; or a composer; a potter; or anyone.'

'Even a physicist?' said Meg. 'I see. Especially a physicist. So you're one of the "try again, fail again, fail better" crew. Without differentiating between science and art. That's excellent.' She laid her knife and fork on the plate and savoured her wine. 'Colin, this has to be the best nosh I've eaten since I don't know when.'

'Good. I'm glad you've enjoyed it. Shall we have our cheese by the fire?'

He put more wood on the embers.

'Why not? But isn't it a bit of a lot dead?' said Meg.

'It needs to breathe, that's all.' He set the cheese board

between them on a stool, and opened a bottle. 'I think you'll find this goes particularly well with Stinking Bishop.'

Flames began to curl.

'It goes a treat,' said Meg.

They sat in silence, watching the fire.

'What a day,' said Meg. 'What a day this has been.'

'I hope it still is,' said Colin.

'I'm thinking,' said Meg. 'I'm thinking about two things in particular.'

'Yes?'

'All those names and initials cut in the soft coloured stone at Castle Rock.'

'They do rather spoil the look of the place, don't they?' said Colin.

'But every one of them meant something when they were cut.'

'I suppose they did.'

'And they do now,' said Meg.

'I take your point, even though I may not agree.'

'Then the carving on the hard bit: the face, labyrinth thingy. That's not vandalism, is it? You'd keep that.'

'Naturally,' said Colin.

'Because it's art? Because it's old? It was a graffito when it was fresh, surely, wasn't it?'

'But for other reasons?'

'Such as?'

'Numen?'

'So how old does a graffito have to be before it's numinous?'

'It may not be age alone,' said Colin. 'I acknowledge that "JH" and "AF" bashed inside a heart give a relationship more permanence than it may have had historically, but perhaps the enigmatic graffito, from the beginning, held more of a charge. And holds it yet. The intensity of the moment may remain.'

'Do you mean that?'

'I do. And why was it not cut on the soft rock? It would have been easier.'

'Mm. But not as enduring. I get you. So it was conscious relative permanence. They knew.'

'I can recommend the Stilton.'

'Thanks.'

'What was the second thing?' said Colin.

'The pebbles in the tunnel. How long have they been shut in that stone?'

'Two hundred and forty-three million years; approximately.'

'Two hundred and forty-three million? How can they bear it?'

'Meg, are you claiming that the inanimate is also sensate?'

'Probably not. More like I'm projecting my own twinge of panic. Like taking your vest off under the bedclothes. But I still feel queasy that those lovely things can't move. Perhaps animism is the human default.'

'But they are moving,' said Colin. 'They can't not be.'

'How do you mean?'

'Do you really want me to tell you?'

'I really want you to tell me.'

'Really really?' His eyes were mischief.

'Really really.'

'Really really really?'

'Really really really.'

'Really really really really really?'

'Colin!'

'Let me refresh your glass. Here comes a party trick.'

'Thanks. That's plenty,' said Meg. 'So what's the party trick?'

'Well now,' said Colin. 'Let's assume that time is linear and unidirectional, otherwise we could soon be lost.'

'You mean it isn't?' said Meg

'Not in my opinion; and thought experiments show this, but by the nature of things not everyone agrees with the premise. I say that time is multi-dimensional and exists in different

83

forms. We've opted for the advancing linear flow, "The Arrow of Time", because it's the most efficient for our needs, and so the easiest to handle, perhaps for Darwinian reasons.'

'Oh yes. Charlie,' said Meg. 'Where should we be without him?'

'Now then. First there's continental drift. Our piece of the Eurasian sheet is currently moving east by east-north-east at a relative speed of one point nine centimetres per year, which gives an absolute velocity of zero point nine five centimetres per year. Clear?'

'Yerrs . . . For the moment. I'll tell you when I'm not. But take it easy.'

'So, I'm the Earth.' Colin spread out his arms, holding his glass in one hand, the bottle in the other. 'The Earth, at our latitude, is rotating at one thousand and four point nine one kilometres per hour, like this.' He began to turn slowly. 'And it's moving in orbit around the Sun at one hundred and seven thousand and four point eight seven kilometres per hour.' Still turning, Colin circled the room. 'I'll keep going, but the rest you'll have to imagine. The relative speeds I'm demonstrating are not accurate, but for illustration only. Right?'

'Right. Just about. But watch your glass.'

'Next, the solar system, let's say this hut, which necessarily would be a lot bigger if it were to scale, is travelling towards the star Lambda Herculis at twenty kilometres per second, and rising at ninety degrees to the plane of the Galaxy at twenty-five thousand one hundred and forty-four point three nine kilometres per hour,' he took a sip of his drink, 'while orbiting the centre of the Galaxy at two hundred kilometres per second. And the Galaxy itself is being drawn by gravitational attraction towards the Local Group at two million one hundred and twenty-one thousand two hundred and ninety-eight point eight kilometres per hour—'

Meg snorted into her wine.

'What's the matter?'

'Can anyone play?'

'I'll ignore that—and ninety-eight point eight kilometres per hour at six hundred kilometres per second relative to the cosmic background of this universe, as opposed to any others that may exist, which—'

'Are you being serious?'

'I am. I would argue it's more than likely—which appears to be expanding currently at eighty kilometres per second per Megapasec; a Megapasec, of course, being three point two six million light years.'

'Of course. How could I be so ignorant? It's common knowledge.' She kept her face straight. 'But which way is Up?'

'These figures are approximate, it goes without saying, and could change, and there are smaller perturbations and turbulations, which we needn't take into account, but they show that your pebble is not in stasis. I think I did that rather well.' Colin plumped down on a chair at the table. 'Don't you? And I'm not even dizzy.'

'I am. I need another drink,' said Meg. 'My brains hurt.'

'Montlouis or Château de Malle?'

'Whatever. Oh, Colin, you really are a tonic! You're too much! You're absurd!' She was spluttering. So was he.

'In short,' said Colin, as he poured, 'if something can happen, it will happen, somehow, somewhere, sometime; though "how", "where" and "when" are dubious words to use in this context, where even time can run backwards.'

'It can?'

'It does. All that's lacking is the clincher proof. But here, on the Edge, is as good a "where" as any. The theory's obvious. We may end at the start. But we may never find an answer, because our brains aren't up to it.'

'I'm not so sure mine is, at any rate,' said Meg.

'And why should it be?' said Colin. 'We're savannah apes.

That's where our brains are at. Why should they need to be equipped to solve the most difficult problems the cosmos may throw at us? Isn't it likely that there are areas as far beyond our comprehension as the theory of relativity is beyond that of an amoeba?'

'Foolish me. Not to think of that.'

'Take tachyons—'

'Oh, I do. Every morning, as regular as clockwork. With my muesli.'

'But it's not so much deep space that concerns me as deep place. Once place is lost, you fall into history.'

'And there's no way out?'

'There's no way out.'

'Mm.'

Colin grinned through the red daub on his face. 'I do hope I haven't ruined your evening. There can be few more dispiriting experiences than being the recipient of detailed but entirely superfluous explanation.'

'Colin, love, you've made my evening,' said Meg. 'And topped it. Strewth. Is it any wonder you're you?' Colin raised his glass. 'But I think I ought to be getting off home now. A girl must work, you know, and I don't want to overstay what's been a great night out. Thank you.'

'Don't mention it. But would you like some coffee or tea before you go?'

'Coffee would be perfect.'

Colin ground the coffee and they drank it by the fire. They said little, but they laughed.

'That's more like it,' said Meg. 'That's the first time I've seen you look even approaching happy.'

'I'm feeling very happy,' said Colin. 'And a bit frivolous.'

'Then that makes two of us. Now I really must be off.'

'Thank you for coming, Meg,' said Colin. He took her hand in both of his. 'I can't tell you how much I've enjoyed it all:

your company, the talk, the friendship; the fellowship. They mean a lot to me.'

'And to me, Colin.'

'May I get you a taxi?'

'No need,' said Meg. 'Bert's outside.'

She would come. She would. She would come soon.

Colin washed up from the meal. Through the window the side of the quarry was green with morning drizzle. He whistled as he dried and polished the glasses.

'The wind, the wind, the wind blows high.

The rain comes pattering down the sky.

She is handsome, she is pretty—'

He put on his head torch, collected the bottles he had not opened, and took them to the adit. He unlocked the iron gate and stepped up into the tunnel. 'The wind, the wind, the wind blows high—' He laid each bottle back in its place. '—She has lovers, one, two, three. Pray can you tell me who is she? Who is she? Who is she?'

Dill doule.

He stopped.

Dill doule. Dill doule.

He looked towards the entrance. The silhouette of a woman was at the step. She was tall and slim, her hair straight to her shoulders. She seemed not to be wearing a coat, and her skirt was knee-length.

'Hello there,' said Colin. 'It's only me. Come in. Come in. Don't stand out in the wet.'

She moved forward to the goblin gold.

'Can you see?'

She did not stop.

'Watch yourself on the wine racks. Wait a moment. I'm coming. I'll be right with you.'

She was beyond the goblin gold and her shape began to block the daylight.

'Wait. The floor's a bit uneven. I'm coming.'

The figure did not stop. There was no reply.

'You'll trip if you're not careful. Stay there.'

A flickering white shone from the quartz pebbles in the wall and roof and outlined her, but it did not show her face. The light stayed with her and died behind her, keeping only to her shape, and she made no noise.

'Who are you?' There was no depth in the figure. It had no features. His torch lit a solid shadow. Colin groped backwards. The figure came on. 'Stop.' He felt the end of the adit against his shoulder. 'Who are you?' She came on. But instead of being larger, the shadow shape was less with every step, shrinking yet keeping its limned form. 'No. Stop. Go away. Go away. I don't want you. Go. Away!—'

It was now the size of a girl, and near.

Dill doule. Dill doule. Dill doule.

She would reach him. She would touch him. Her small arms lifted.

'No!'

Colin pulled a full rack of wine across from the wall, and the bottles fell, smashing in rainbows, fragments lancing his mind. He roared. He screamed. The howl tore his chest, and he ran for the daylight down the adit, over the broken glass.

He slammed the hut door behind him and bolted it. He snatched the telephone. 'Yes, Colin.' The connection was open.

'Help.'

'Stay where you are. I'll raise Bert. He'll be with you as soon as he can. Stay where you are.' The connection went dead.

Colin looked from the window. The quarry was empty. The adit was blank. He unfastened the door and made for the quarry entrance, walking quickly, watching behind him.

'Hello, Col. You shouldn't have done that. You really shouldn't

88

have done that. You know what happens when men look back. I told you. I did.'

The voice was all about him. He was between the dishes.

'You!' He ran to the focus. He whispered. 'Is it you?'

'Oh, Col. Who else were you expecting? I told you. I did tell you. Didn't I? I told you she'd get you. And this time I couldn't stop her. You say you don't want me now. You say go away. And you let her paint your face. Silly boy. Naughty. Need a smack. You've still got some of that red stuff in your beard. Never mind. Shall I sing you a song? I'll sing you a song.'

'Wait. I'm sorry. I didn't know it was you.'

'Oh yes you did. Too late. Listen. Such a pretty song. Isn't it a pretty song?'

'Please.'

'Dill doule for Colin. Colin is dead and gone.'

'What?'

'Left his life all alone, all his work undone.'

'No.'

'Dill doule. Dill doule.'

'Please.'

'Where shall we bury him? Carry him to Ludchurch.
By his grandfathers' cave grows holly, grows the birch.
Dill doule. Dill doule.'

'Stop.'

'Make the cave wide and deep. Strew it with flowers.
Toll the bell, toll the bell, twenty-four hours.
Dill doule. Dill doule. Dill doule. Dill doule. Dill doule.'

'No.'

'Dill doule. Dill doule. Dill doule. Dill doule. Dill doule. Dill doule. Dill doule. Dill doule. Dill doule. Dill doule.'

He ran to the other dish and put his ear at the focus.

'Dill doule. Dill doule. Dill doule.'

He ran between.

'Dill doule. Dill doule.'

He ran out of the ambient line. Silence.

Colin faced the adit. The thick liquid had reached the step and was trickling from the opening into the quarry. The Edge was bleeding more than had been spilt. It welled over the lip and surged and slopped.

Colin ran. He ran out of the quarry onto the track and to the road. A car was turning in and he fell across the bonnet.

'Eh up, our Colin,' said Bert. 'Well I never. You're a sight for sore eyes. You are that. Let's be having you. Not much of a day, is it? I could make better weather meself.'

The wild weathers of the world passed and the day lengthened in the bidding sun. But the woman did not come. Soon the clonter of the river would start and she could not cross. He hewed a holly branch to hold him and trimmed it and took the last of the food, and set out over the ice to fetch her.

He climbed towards the Tor of Ghosts from where he could see all the world that was.

He met spirits on the high fell; wolves, too, and bulls and bears and boars; but the way was longer than before and the land shifted under him, and the light around. He saw things that he could not tell: things that wound their tails round knolls, and the knars were big men that were not there. He dreamed horrors as he walked.

And the wind grew worse. Each hill had a hood, a huge hackle of mist, and the cold clear rain that shed from the clouds was ice when it hit. He should have been dead of the sleet; but Ludcruck held. The clamour of the cranes and the beasts reached out and kept him for this journey.

So. It was the morning when he woke and left the hole where he had slept and he followed a clough into a wood with banks on each side and the tangled trees were hung with skins of moss and on the twigs birds cried for pain of the cold. But it was shelter from the wind as he climbed, until he came out on

90

a moor and the white snow lay beside. The sky was red, and the sun shone on the Tor of Ghosts above him.

He climbed towards the ridge of the Tor, leaning on the branch, and however far he climbed the ridge came no nearer. But he knew it was the trick of the Tor, so that only the strong mind would gain the peak. Behind him billowed to the Motherworld.

The sun was as high as it reached at that season, and he saw the ridge grow nearer and felt the ground ease under his branch. The wind had dropped. The ridge was before him. The rocks of the Tor were its crest, and he stepped onto them.

Below him lay all that was. He looked across to the hills that kept the Flatlands from falling into the sky. And in that distance there was no one. He called to the woman, but she did not answer. The bone of the Mother was pure, but his hand had not cut true. He had waited too long. Now he was not singer, not dancer, but the meat of pain.

He cramped on the rock of the Tor and wept. Then, because his head was low, he saw nearer, through the water of his eyes, the Hill of Death and Life stretching into the Flatlands. And from the Hill smoke rose in the still air.

He pulled himself by the holly to stand and look again. It was the smoke of one fire. He called to it. It did not tell him. But he knew. The woman had come. He felt life, and danced and sang about the branch.

Wolf! Wolf! Grey Wolf! I am calling for you!

Far away the Grey Wolf heard and came.

Here am I, the Grey Wolf.

The smoke on the Hill of Death and Life!

That is Trouble. The Trouble has come.

Wolf. Wolf. Grey Wolf. It is the woman. Take me up on your shoulder and run higher than the trees, lower than the clouds. Let each leap measure a mile and from your feet flints fly, springs sprout, lake surge and mix with gravel dirt, birch bend to the ground. Make hare crouch, boar bristle, crow call, owl wake, and stag begin to bell until I reach her.

I shall not, and I will not. I come three times. No more.

Then what is there to do?

That will I tell you. Go down from here and take the Stone. Then walk on the blood of your feet to the Hill of Death and Life.

But the Stone is the birth of night and the womb of being. Nothing before it was made, and with it all things were made. It lies in Ludcruck; and the river runs beneath. If I take it, all things must end.

Long hair, short wit. I the Grey Wolf am speaking. Do it.

Is there no other way?

No other. Live long. Die well. But me you shall see no more.

The Grey Wolf struck the damp earth and was gone.

Colin crouched in the chair, his knees drawn up to his chest, one hand over his eyes, the thumb of the other sideways between his teeth.

'Go to where the pain is most and say what it tells you.'

'No. Not that. Not that again. It's too embarrassing. Infantile.'

'Go to where the pain is most and say what it tells you.'

He rocked in the chair. Meg was silent.

'I—'

She did not speak.

'I—'

A bird was outside the window.

'House sparrow. *Passer domesticus*. It has brown and grey plumage. Feeds on seeds and insects.'

Meg did not answer.

'It has a small, round head and a simple song of one or a series of cheeps or chirrups notes, as you can hear.'

No reply. He bit on his hand.

'I—Blood! Blood!'

'Nothing wrong with a spot of blood,' said Meg. 'You'll live. Do you want a plaster?'

'From the rock!'

'So?'

'I'm running. She's speaking. She's speaking to me. Says you've got me. She can't stop you. I'm naughty. Dirty. Horrid. Need a smack.'

'They can get peevish,' said Meg. 'Go on.'

'She's singing. Singing a song.'

'What about?'

'Me. I'm no good. Finished. Out. Dead.'

'Oh, she's being a little madam, this one,' said Meg.

'Going to bury me.'

'Where?'

'Ludchurch. I don't know what she means. What's Ludchurch? Then Bert comes.'

'And now you're here, safe and sound,' said Meg. 'I'm afraid that's not enough, darling. What's really hurting? What's really bugging you?'

'Nothing. Nothing else.'

'OK. Colin. Let's try again. What's the worst thing that happens? I don't need to know what she says. What's the worst thing she does?'

'No.'

'Speak it.'

'No.'

'Right, then. If that's how you are,' said Meg, 'I can't help. You have to do it for yourself. I can't kiss it better.'

'You promised not to ditch me.'

'I'm not ditching you, treasure. But until you quit dodging you're a waste of space.'

'What do you want?' said Colin.

'I want you to go to what scares you most.'

Colin uncovered his eyes.

'I'll be all right?'

'You'll be all right.'

'Promise?'

'No.'

'Her arms. Her hands. Reaching. To get me.'

'She's not trying to get you, Colin. She's a child. She wants to be picked up. She wants you to pick her up. To hold her.'

'Me?'

'I told you. She hurts, too. She's scared.'

'What am I going to do?'

'Give her another chance.'

'How? What do you mean?'

'It's down to you. But I suggest you try; and soon. She doesn't mean to, but she's turning into a right bitch. And you're not helping.'

'I don't know what to do.'

'You'll find out,' said Meg. 'Just remember how scared she is; how scared you both are. Help her grow up.'

The smoke rose from the Hill of Death and Life but did not answer. He left the rocks of the Tor and went down.

His legs jarred. Without the holly he could not have walked, and he fell as his grip gave to the pain. When he reached the clough the tangled trees were a net through which he had to thrust. He could not pull on them as he had on the way up.

The sun dropped, and it was by the light of the stars that he followed his tracks to the hole in the snow; and ate; and slept.

'Hi, Colin. Sit down.'

'I need to talk.'

'Fire away.'

'No. I need to tell you. I want to tell you something. I want you to listen.'

'So what's different?'

'I've made the biggest mistake of my life.'

'I do that every day,' said Meg. 'Join the club.'

'No. I can't go on. I have to resign my post.'

'Oh, don't be such a drama queen. What's the hoo-ha?'

'It's about my sister.'

'Is it, now? I'm all ears.'

'It started three years ago.'

'What did?'

'You know I've said I get flashbacks, and they don't add up?'

'Mm.'

'I had the same flashback three times, close together.'

'Were you awake or dreaming?'

'Both,' said Colin.

'Can you tell the difference?'

'Dreams are more real.'

'You're learning,' said Meg. 'Go on.'

'It hadn't happened before. Flashbacks don't repeat. Well, not often. But these did. They became real, waking or sleeping.'

'Tell me.'

'I've not told anyone. I thought it was true. I knew it was true. But I knew if I said anything, or applied for a grant, I could lose my job. But I needed my job to prove I was right. Without the telescope I couldn't find her.'

'What were the flashbacks?'

'I saw her. I saw my twin. I saw her riding; riding a horse. M45.'

'On a motorway? That is odd. Especially when you're awake.'

'Sorry. Messier enumeration. The Pleiades. I saw her ride into the Pleiades. I saw.'

'You're an astronomer, honeybundle, not a bloody poet. Then again, come to think of it, I suppose you're both.'

'I am what I am,' said Colin. 'We think we understand. But we don't. Out there everything's possible. It's not "either or".

95

The more we look the more we find. What did I say about the carving on Castle Rock?'

'But constellations are subjective patterns of random stars. Aren't they?'

'The Pleiades are a discrete asterism. It's all one. I saw her ride.'

'Did you see her face?'

'—No. But it was her.'

'How far off are the Pleiades?' said Meg.

'About four hundred and forty light years.'

'Then she can't be there yet.'

'When time is linear only,' said Colin. 'But when it isn't . . .'

'Hang about,' said Meg. 'I'm not used to playing in your backyard. You'll have to be patient.'

'I am the patient,' said Colin.

'It's not funny, my lad. Don't muck around with this.'

'You have to understand,' said Colin. 'There can be more than one answer. There could be an infinity of answers. Truth isn't fixed. Consider the Ex Africa hypothesis.'

'I'm considering it, my heart.'

'Allowing for cultural change, wherever we go in the world people tend to see the same things in the sky, even though they seldom look like what they're called. Orion is a hunter. Ursa Major is a predator, most often a bear. Taurus is a bull. Cygnus is a bird, usually one of the anseriformes; or *Grus grus*, a crane. And the Pleiades are a band of women, typically, or maidens, escaping pursuit. Did *Homo sapiens sapiens* see all this and take it with him out of the Rift Valley? If so, the urgency must have been strong, even of evolutionary significance, at the global dispersal.'

'So what's your point?' said Meg. 'Slow down. You are distinctly high today.'

'Both systems can be real, but both are models. You can't, or shouldn't, confuse them. I did.'

'Hey now, kiddo,' said Meg. 'Are you, an astrophysicist, saying that mythology and science have equal validity?'

'I'm saying they could have. There may be truth in fairy tales. My mistake was to mix them.'

'Too right,' said Meg. '"Always believe the fairy tales. What were the fairy tales, they will come true." That's what they say in Russia.'

'Oh, thank goodness. At least you understand,' said Colin. 'I thought you wouldn't. I've been using the telescope to find a myth, an object to trace a metaphor. They may both be real, but if so they occupy different dimensions.'

'Chasing love with a scalpel?'

'Yes.'

'And metaphor, not simile?'

'Yes.'

'OK. I'll buy metaphor, but simile's a cop-out used by scaredycats who won't commit to anything. Simile's for cowards. So where's your reality?'

'Faith is the only truth. Belief the reality. Until you're inconsistent.'

'Ever thought of having my job?' said Meg. 'You'd go down a storm.'

'You've decided I'm mad,' said Colin.

'Oh my giddy aunt! I'll tell you when you are.'

'Promise truly scout's honour?'

'Promise truly scout's honour.'

'I'm depending on you, Meg.'

'Unwise. Only you can get you back on track. How often must I say that?'

'I need your word.'

'You've got it. That's the easy bit.'

'But I can't stay at the telescope. I've abused my contract. I've let everyone down.'

'Stop being such a wazzock,' said Meg. 'And don't play the

martyr with me, my lad. You're needed, Colin. You may be off the wall, but you're creatively off it, and we don't get many of your kind to the pound.'

When at last he came to the lodge he blew a fire heap and he lay for one day. He lay for two days. He lay for three. He unlooped a fox from a snare and ate. Then he lay by the fire heap until there was no more wood to feed it. He took a blade and cut holly from the cliffs in strands that grew along the rocks; and he wove a ladder. The branches flexed, but each bend and twist used all his will, and each day he worked less, and curled with his fingers bent into him for warmth to work the next.

It was enough.

He linked the holly to his foot and went by the nooks of the dead. The holly followed. The seam of grit clenched his neck. The clamour of the beasts was stilled, and he saw that their lines were dying because he had not cut them fresh. He came to the brink of the great cave and hung the holly on a spur and let it down. He held the lamp and began to climb. The leaf spikes counted the rungs to the last step and the rock floor above the shining waters.

His feet trod the chippings of the Stone. The shards bit through to his feet and his knees would not bear the dance. The Stone lay black. He eased himself to lodge on the edges of the flakes and set the lamp apart so that it did not slight the Stone. He could not dance, but he could sing. He rested on his arms, and looked down into the Stone. The Stone took him and gave him songs that he had not learnt, and the dark was all that he could see. It filled his eyes. He sang. And with each song the dark that was all grew darker still. It had no depth, but he moved into it, pulled by the singing into noth-ingness that turned about him as it drew him on.

He rushed at the night; but the singing held him. If this was

98

death, he had no fear. He came to where it could not be more black. Yet still he sank into the Stone.

The dark was spent, and below him he saw a point. He lay in Ludcruck above the Stone and of it, and beyond the spinning dark he entered light. He saw the blackness break, and on the other side was sky, still night, but flecked with stars.

He sang.

The light was stars and more than stars. There were pools that swirled, and in them suns. The pools and stars had no end. They fled for ever and there were no songs to fetch them. But he had seen.

The whole Stone blazed. Ludcruck was every light. He shut his eyes against the pain, and when he opened them the Stone was small, lit by the lamp.

He put out a hand and lifted the Stone. It fitted his palm and his fingers closed around. The smooth side told his fingers where to sit, and where it had been shaped a hard sharp edge sat ready to be used for the work it had to do to make the world. He took it, the little thing that held the stars, and climbed past the beasts, along the seam of grit, by the nooks of the dead, into the day.

'Hi, Colin. Come in. Sit down. Have some water. But please try not to smash the glass this time.'

'Why? What's the matter?'

'I've been keeping something back,' said Meg, 'in the hope it wouldn't be necessary and you'd work it out for yourself.'

'What? You're frightening me.'

'Don't be scared. I want to help. But I need your help, too. It may hurt.'

'What is it?'

'As soon as you said your sister was your twin I had a firm date, so I went to the Register of Births, Marriages and Deaths. Did you ever do that?'

'No. There wasn't any need to. I knew.'

'You "knew". But wasn't it you told me what a waste of a fart it is to think you "know"?'

Colin was silent.

'So I went to the Register,' said Meg. 'And there she was, without any doubt. You can drop the Missing syndrome. You had a twin. She was real.'

'I told you,' said Colin. 'Where is she?'

'I said "had".'

'But I have! She's real! I said!'

'She was,' said Meg. 'Do you want me to go on?'

'Don't keep putting her into the past! She talks to me!'

'I know she does, love.'

'You're saying I'm mad. You are.'

'Not yet. Now do you want to hear me, or do you not want to hear me?'

'I want to hear you.'

'OK. But no clever stuff, please, Colin. No tachywhatsits, thank you. Let's keep to pen and paper. All right?'

'All right.'

'Right.'

'I need the lavatory,' said Colin.

'You know where it is.'

He came back and sat on the front edge of the chair. Meg opened a file.

'You, Colin Whisterfield, male, together with your female twin—'

'No!'

'What's the matter?'

'Not her name!'

'Why?' said Meg.

'You don't need to tell me her name!'

'You said you couldn't remember.'

'I lied! You don't need to tell me!'

'Why not?'

'It's private!'

'Not on this certificate, it isn't. Colin. It's in the public domain.'

'I don't care! We're private!'

'That just about wraps it up, then,' said Meg. 'You're showing patent hysteria. Or do you want to know what happened, if you don't know already?'

'"Happened"?' said Colin. 'What do you mean?'

'I'm trying to work through your isolated retrograde amnesia. If it's too much pain, leave it for now. We can have a go another day.'

'No. Sorry. Now. I'll try.'

'No "sorries",' said Meg. 'But if you can try, it may help.'

'What do you want?'

'A few questions and answers.'

'I'll try.'

'Good lad. First. Did the Mossocks have a horse?'

'Oh, yes,' said Colin. 'He was a grey Shire. Called Prince. He pulled the cart on Fridays. The Mossocks used to go to the village, selling eggs and poultry and vegetables. There were regular customers. Prince didn't need telling. He knew which houses to stop at. And he'd wait. That was when it was a genuine village, with people and real shops. No black cars.'

'What happened to Prince?'

'He was put down when the farm was sold. He'd been at pasture for years. He was a smashing horse.'

'I bet he was. Did you ride him?'

'Not really. He was too big; seventeen hands. And he didn't have a saddle. But I liked to climb up and sit on his back and walk him round the fields.'

'Could you have fitted a bridle on him?'

'Yes. There were reins. And a bridle.'

'OK,' said Meg. 'Thanks.'

'Why are you asking?' said Colin. 'What have you got there?'

'A copy of a report.'

'May I see it?'

'Not yet.'

'Why not?'

'It may be too much for you, and it wouldn't help me. It's tough reading. Please be patient, love, and let me do it my way.'

Colin slumped in the chair, his head back, watching Meg.

'At twenty past midnight,' said Meg, 'and I'm condensing this, on the twenty-second of November, when you were twelve years old, the Mossocks alerted the police that your sister and the horse were missing.

'The Mossocks said they had been woken by the dog barking and the noise of hooves in the yard. When they went to look they found the stable empty and the road gate open. Your sister's hat was in the lane, and the bridle wasn't on its peg, though the rest of the harness was there. She wasn't in her room, and her clothes and coat had gone. Her pyjamas were by the bed.'

'Where was I?'

'Asleep in the next room. Do you remember any of this? Anything? An echo? An atmosphere? Police? Anything?'

'No. I need a map,' said Colin. 'Now.'

'Help yourself,' said Meg, and passed him a computer.

'It was zero zero twenty of the twenty-second of November,' said Colin. 'You're sure?'

'That's what it says here.'

'What happened?'

'The police called out patrols, but didn't find a thing until daylight,' said Meg.

'And then?'

'The next bit's not easy.'

'I'm all right. I'm all right.'

'Sure?'

'Yes. Tell me.'

'There were traces of hoof prints crossing the fields, and they were all a match of those that had left the yard.'

'Then?'

'Nothing. Until a farmer phoned in from Redesmere.'

'Yes.' Colin was tapping the computer keys. 'Yes.'

'Do you want a break?' said Meg.

'No. Don't stop. It's making sense.'

'He reported that there was a horse, a grey Shire, on an island in the mere. He'd gone down to the mere and had seen hoof prints which ended in the water.'

'Yes. There is an island.'

'The horse must have swum.'

'Yes.'

'The police went out with a vet and brought the horse back unharmed. The Mossocks identified it; and the bridle. But there was no girl. Are you all right, Colin?'

'Yes. Go on.'

'Frogmen made a fingertip search, and the mere was dragged; and the surrounding fields and rhododendrons were searched. No one had left the mere, and nothing was found. This is the coroner's report. I'm sorry, love.'

'No. No,' said Colin. 'Wait.' He took a calculator from his pocket. 'Wait. Yes! Oh, Meg!'

'What?'

'The Pleiades culminate at midnight of the twenty-first of November!'

'I don't get you. What's "culminate"?'

'The highest point reached on the meridian in the year,' said Colin. 'That's why she rode! She followed! By the time she got to Redesmere they were reflected in the water. Meg! She had to! She made it!'

'But why?' said Meg.

'She had to.'

'And why the Pleiades?'

'Ex Africa,' said Colin. 'The Pleiades are so often the refuge of women and maidens.'

'Refuge from what?'

'Threat of one kind or another. Usually pursuit.'

'Women and maidens,' said Meg. 'But not girls, children?'

'Not that I know of,' said Colin. 'I'm not an expert.'

'The threat makes sense. It's obvious.'

'How?' said Colin.

'Menarche. Now she's adult. But she's immature. So are you. Is that why she's back? She needs help. So do you. Riddle me that.'

He wrapped the Stone and the blades in a skin of birch bark, and bound them with twined strands of his hair and went from Ludcruck down by the easy ways. He saw the Hill of Death and Life. The smoke still rose. Above him the cranes called on their path back to the Flatlands, but he could not join them. He walked on the blood of his feet with the holly branch, a journey that once he could do in a day; but now he had to rest. After the night he went down to the Eelstream, a long walk, and here the ice was breaking and he had to cross the floes. They cracked under him and if they turned over he would die. He tapped his way, listening to the ice. Many times only the holly kept him, but he crossed, and ahead was the clear way to the Hill. The frost had gone from the land. The ground pulled at him and he waded sludge.

On the third day, he came to the Hill, and went about its flanks to where the spirit colours lay in bands among the rocks. He took the red earth, the blue earth, the green earth and painted his face to sing strong. Then he climbed to the Point of Storms and looked across the curve between the two spurs of the Hill. The smoke rose by the Great Rock, but he could not see or hear what made it.

So he went around the curve, keeping to the scrub of birch. On one side the Hill smoothed away into the Flatlands to where the sun reached its highest, and on the other the land dropped sheer to a mire that, after winter, glimmered death.

He went quietly, pausing, listening, so as not to frighten her. He stopped. There was noise. The sound of a hammer on flint. Then silence. Then more blows, but now with bone. She had brought flint with her from wherever she had come. There was no flint on the Hill, nor any in the world, except flakes in Ludcruck from when the spirits had first struck blades. If the woman was a spirit there could be no child. He worked the red earth across his brow for better strength, and went on.

He listened. The flint sang, but now he could tell that it was not one but three. Three hands were working together; living or spirit hands. He could not tell.

Are you people or ghosts?

There was no answer.

He came to the Great Rock. The smoke rose from the other side. He lay and crawled. Something laughed. Again. It was a woman, not a spirit. Another laugh. Then mouths made sounds. They were not words but chopped noise. And then a cry that was a voice. It was a cry for milk, as he had heard in Ludcruck before the ice fell.

Fear sat upon his neck. He moved forward and sideways to look past the Great Rock. And the fear went onto his tongue for what he saw, and made him rise.

They were women. One was putting a child to a breast. They were women, but they were not people. They were three but they were only one. He could not make them more. The nose of each was in the middle of the face. They had two eyes, level and the same on either side of the nose. Each mouth was straight, under the nose; the chin the same beneath. There was no difference. The feeding woman had bared her hands. Each had four fingers and one thumb.

What are you?

They could not hear. He spoke with open voice.

'What are you?'

They looked, and screamed and made more noise. They were by a fire before a shelter in a sloping cliff, with hides hanging at the front and weighted with stones. One of the women lifted a spear. Its point was none he knew, and it had small blades along its shaft, but it would kill. Another took a brand from the fire and held it towards him. They screamed again.

'I am no harm,' he said. 'I sang for a woman to make a child to learn to sing and dance and cut to free the life in Ludcruck. You have come. But what are you?'

He moved forward on the holly.

They huddled and screamed again. He stopped.

'I am no harm.'

There was a crashing in the scrub beyond, and five men came running. They were men because of their beards, but all their faces, as the women, were one. Each had a wolf, and only by them could he tell each from another apart.

The wolves snarled towards him, but when he looked into their eyes he saw that their spirits were broken. And they saw his eye and its power, and turned and went to the men.

The men too made noise, and one drew back a spear to throw.

'I am no harm.'

But they could not hear. He held out the blade that had cut the veil in Ludcruck.

'I brought you with this.'

The man lowered his spear and moved forward slowly. He took the blade, then showed it to the others. They made noise, and the women were still.

The man came, and he put a hand on the hand that held the holly. The weight was too much. His strength had kept the journey. Now it was gone, and he fell. The world was ended.

106

The dream was done. With his last force he lifted the Stone and showed it for the man.

The man took the Stone and looked close at the blackness and at the working. Behind him there was a spirit face, new in the Rock.

'Hi, Colin,' said Owen. 'How's your mother's rag arm?'

'Is R.T. in?'

'If he's not out.'

'Anyone with him?'

'Don't think so.'

Colin picked up the telephone.

'R.T.? Colin here. Would it be possible to have a word with you? Now. Thanks. Thank you very much.'

'What's to do?' said Owen.

'Nothing.'

'Buck up, youth. It might never happen.'

'It already has,' said Colin.

He left the control room and went to the Director's door and knocked.

'Yes, Whisterfield.'

Colin opened the door. The Director was at his desk.

'Come in, my boy. What may I do for you?'

Colin shut the door and stayed by it.

'Come in. Come in. Take a seat.'

'I'd rather stand. R.T., I want to apologise.'

'Apologise for what?'

'Everything. I've wasted your time. I've wasted the budget, the telescope. Everything. I thought I was right. I was wrong. Completely wrong. I didn't need them to find the solution. All it took was a pocket calculator and a map. I'm sorry.'

'You are describing research,' said the Director. 'No one is right at once. You may see the answer in an instant, but finding and then clarifying the question can be another matter entirely.

You speak as though you are on the edge of discovery. Trust me. I have heard this before. I have said it myself. I know how you feel.'

Colin shook his head and stepped forward. He took an envelope out of his pocket and put it on the desk.

'I want you to accept my resignation. With immediate effect. My desk will be cleared by the end of today. I am so very sorry.'

'Your behaviour is impractical and ridiculous,' said the Director. 'Sit down.'

'There's nothing more to be said. My work is pointless.'

'Look here, Whisterfield,' said the Director. 'It is you that are wrong, not your work. Your work, until you became ill, and that will surely pass, has been the most promising I have known in my lifetime. My dear boy, you have it in you to go beyond the Singularity. Your vision could take us to our next understanding.'

'I'm sorry,' said Colin. 'Forgive me. I must.' He turned and left the room and closed the door. He went to his office and sat. He pulled open the drawers of his desk and stared at them. He felt an empty cold and heard silence.

The air moved behind him and a hand put the envelope, unopened, by his elbow and laid something on it and withdrew.

Colin looked. The envelope was under the Director's black stone paperweight. Colin looked at the curve and the scars of the stone that swept to make a sharp edge of one side and the narrow flaking that drew the end to a point.

He took the stone in his hand, which fitted on the smoothness so that the edge was between fingers and thumb and the point below. He felt; and he saw. Colin stood, kicked the chair aside, and ran.

'R.T.! Where did you get this? Where?'

'I found it.'

'Don't you know what it is?' Colin was shouting quietly.

'It is a comforting object to hold,' said the Director, 'and I think you may benefit from it now more than I. Beyond that, it is a stone. A tactile stone. But a stone nonetheless.'

'It's Abbevillian! Or Acheulian! Non-derived! Pre-Anglian! MIS 13!'

'You must help me there, I'm afraid.'

'*Homo erectus*, or *heidelbergensis*!'

'I still do not understand your excitement, Whisterfield. What is the matter?'

'Where did you get it?'

'Strange that you should ask that. When I decided, younger than you, to proceed with my "contraption", as you call it, after the survey had defined the mid point under the dish I took a divot out with a spade to mark the moment, and the stone was lying on the sand beneath. I picked it up and have kept it out of sentiment.'

'But it shouldn't be here!'

'And why not?'

'It couldn't have survived the climatic conditions! The sands are recent: Holocene: post-glacial. This is an artefact: five ice ages and half a million years old!'

He woke. The sky was above and the world swayed under him. He was lying on thongs lashed between poles, and four men were carrying him on their shoulders. He heard their breath. The holly was along his body and his arms crossed over it. In one hand he held the white blade and in the other the Stone. He did not have the strength to move or to look. He lay lulled in the rhythm of the breathing and the thongs, moving in and out of sleep, weary beyond fear.

The men stopped and set him down. He could not see the sky, but there was warmth and smoke. He turned his head. There was a man sitting over him, his face no different from the others, but painted green, red and blue; and in his eyes there was a light theirs did not have, and the smoke was sweet.

What are you? The man spoke straight, without sound.

I dream in Ludcruck.

What is Ludcruck? said the other.

It is the cave of the world.

The other looked down and into him.

I see it. Why are you here?

To fetch the woman I cut from the veil of the rock.

Why did you cut?

To send her spirit out so that she would come to make the child for me to teach to dance and sing and dream to free the beasts within the rock to fill the world.

Have you found her?

She is not here. There are only people horrible to see.

Where are your Stories? said the other.

I cannot tell them. My head is a cloud.

A hand lifted him, and another put something hard between his teeth and dripped water from it. Then a mouth, with no beard, came and a tongue fed him warm meat that he did not need to chew, and the hand came again for him to drink; and the mouth again; and the water. And he slept.

'The wind, the wind, the wind blows high.
The rain comes pattering down the sky.
She is handsome, she is pretty,
She is the girl of the windy city.
She has lovers, one, two, three;
Pray will you tell me who is she?
Pray will you tell me who is she?
Pray will you tell me who is she?
Pray will you tell me who is she?
Pray will you tell me who is she?
Who is she?

Who is she?

Who is she?'

Colin turned in his bunk. 'I don't understand.'

'Pray will you tell me?

Pray will you tell me?

Pray will you tell me?'

'I can't hear you.'

'Pray will you tell?

Pray will you tell?

Pray will you?'

'Meg.'

'Pray.'

Where are your Stories?

The man with light in his eyes sat over him, and the smoke was sweet. The cloud moved from his head.

Here is my Story.

In the Beginning was Crane. It opened its wings. And that above it called Sky, and that below it called Earth. The wings lifted Sky from Earth and flew between to hold them apart. And Crane laid a black Egg and made it with its beak to be a Stone. And when the Stone was made Crane breathed on the flakes that it had shed and said: Be spirits. Take the Stone and with it shape the world. Give mountains and rivers and waters.

And Crane laid another Egg and opened it and said to the yolk: Be Sun, and give light. And it said to the water about the yolk: Be Moon, so that when Sun sleeps you will give light. And because you held Sun inside the Egg you are its mother and will live for ever; but you will remember how you gave birth, and each month you will grow big and then small and then rest for three nights before you grow again. And so that there will be no dark, I shall take the shell and make it into pieces and call them stars and give them spirits and shapes to light the world. And from the skin of the Egg I shall make a

111

mighty Spirit to send out eagles from its head to feed the stars. And I shall put people to walk the earth, and make beasts that they may hunt. And so that they may have spears to hunt with and blades to cut, I shall shape a Mother of rock from a bone of Moon and set it in the hills. And the people shall come and sing and dance and tell stories of the Beginning and dream, so that she will let them take of the bone, and live.

Then Crane came down to the world and broke the loud crag with its beak and opened it to the waters below and called it Ludcruck. And in the lowmost cavern it put the Stone and the spirits around it to take the Stone and make all that would be.

Then Crane went back to fly for ever so that Earth and Sky should stand apart and life could live.

That is my Story.

It is a true Story, said the other.

Colin rang the doorbell.

'Good morning, Professor Whisterfield. Is Doctor Massey expecting you?'

'No, she isn't. It's a social call. A very important social call. Very.'

'Please come in, Professor. Would you excuse me a moment, please? I'll see if the Doctor's available.'

'She's got to be. Tell her who it is. Tell her. Now. Tell her it's urgent. It's me. Tell her.'

Colin paced the room. He counted the knots on the fringe of the carpet. He counted the colours. He counted the right angles in the design. He counted the wear.

'What do you want, Colin?' said Meg. She was in the library doorway.

'Amazing. Meg. Amazing.'

'So, because you decide to be amazing, the rest of the world has to stop and listen to you.'

'You'll be astonished.'

'It can't wait, can it? It may be the most critical moment of the year, two patients have topped themselves, the cat's got fleas, the house is on fire, the samovar is empty and the old pig has died; but tomorrow won't do. The little boy has to have attention now.'

'Yes. Now. It's incredible.'

'If it can't be believed, then what's the point?' said Meg. 'Oh, come on in. But you are more than a tad manic, you know that?'

Colin went to the low table by the hearth, threw the box of tissues into the chair and skewed the table to the chaise longue. He put a cushion on the table.

'Sit down, here, Meg. Sit down. Sit down! Sit!'

Meg sat on the chaise longue and Colin sat beside her. He reached into his pocket and took out a folded handkerchief, laid it on the cushion, and opened it.

'There.'

'Oh, great,' said Meg. 'Terrific. You've made my day.'

The black stone lay on the white linen.

'Look at it,' said Colin. 'Don't you see what it is?'

'Yes,' said Meg. 'I see it. I see a pebble.'

'Meg!'

'OK. A big pebble.'

'Meg!'

'OK. A big black pebble.'

'Meg!'

'OK. A chipped big black pebble. A lump of rock.'

'Meg! Look! It's a Lower Palaeolithic Abbevillian hand axe!'

'It is? You astound me, Colin.'

'Hold it. Feel it. Look at it. But keep it over the cushion.'

Meg took the stone in her hand.

'Turn it. It'll tell you.'

Meg moved the stone around in her palm and fingers.

113

'Good grief. It's alive.'

'It is! You can feel it!'

The stone fitted her hand. The smooth curves were against her skin. The rough serrations were outside her thumb and fingers, and the fluted point below.

'Is it human?' she said.

'Hominin. Just about,' said Colin. '*Homo erectus*, perhaps, or *Homo heidelbergensis*; but definitely not *sapiens* or *sapiens sapiens*.'

'Lower Palaeolithic?' said Meg. 'So how old are we talking here?'

'About half a million years.'

'"About"?'

'It's impossible to be more accurate. There's no context.'

'Where did you find it?'

'I didn't. R.T., the Director, he dug it up when he was planning the telescope. It was directly beneath where the light of the focus would be when it's in the zenith.'

'Mm. That is remarkable,' said Meg. 'It is amazing. I agree.'

'You don't know how much,' said Colin. 'It's half a million years old, but he found it under the turf, on top of soil that's only ten thousand, at most.'

'How do you account for that?'

'I can't. It shouldn't have been there.'

'Let's get real,' said Meg. 'I grant you it handles as if it's a tool, but are you sure it's not natural?'

'I'm positive. It's a cobble made from a flake. It has smooth natural facets and naturally rounded butt, all showing derived features, which means at one time it was rolling around in water; a brook or river, say. Then someone picked it up; chose it; worked it. The end has been pointed, by pressure or indirect percussion, though that, I must say, is unusual, and a sinuous edge has been formed through bifacial chipping and step flaking to give a triangular section. The opposite edge has been heavily blunted. All the flake scars appear to be contemporaneous and non-derived. Secondary silication of the scars is uniform and complete. Somehow it has been protected from the Anglian and subsequent glaciations. It shouldn't be possible for it to have survived here. Yet it has. Of that there can be no doubt.'

Meg turned the stone over and over in her hand. 'OK,' she said. 'I don't get the technical malarky, but it sits one way, and one way only, and right.'

'I told you it would tell you,' said Colin.

'Yep. I wasn't tuned in. I am now. You've converted me. "This stone is poor, and cheap in price; spurned by fools, loved more by the wise."'

'Sorry?' said Colin.

'I'm translating. You say you're crap at Latin. Well, this asks the Grail Question. And, come to think of it, the Grail can be a stone, too.'

'I don't understand what it is you're saying.'

'You don't understand? That's a relief. I was beginning to feel a bit of a bozo.'

'I've heard of it, but I don't know what it is,' said Colin. 'The Question.'

'"What is this thing? What does it mean? Whom does it serve?" If those mediaeval retarded adolescents of the Round Table hadn't been so anally retentive but had asked the Question straight off, a lot of knights would have been out of a job quick smart.'

Meg turned the stone.

'That's just what R.T. used to do,' said Colin. 'He found it comforting. But he couldn't see that it was anything more than what he called "tactile".'

'I know what he meant,' said Meg. 'It's a feely. Yes. Better than worry beads, any day. There could be quite a market. The way the smooth goes into the sharp and out again; and the ripples in the scars; like sea shells.'

'That's the conchoidal fracture,' said Colin.

'And how've you come by it?' said Meg.

'R.T. gave it to me.'

'Gave it to you? Why?'

'He said I had more need of it now than he had.'

'Oh? How's that?'

'I resigned from my post.'

'Shit and derision. Colin? What did I tell you? I can't be doing with martyrs. Is this how you fail better? Have you not got one single ounce of gumption in you?'

'I know. But I felt I must. Had to. Immediately. But he wouldn't accept it.'

'I should think not. You prannock. You total pillock.'

'He gave me this instead.'

'Good on him. Did you tell him what it was?'

'I tried to tell him, but he didn't seem to be interested.'

'Wise man.' She turned the stone. 'How black is that?'

'Black blacker than black,' said Colin. 'Black as carbon; though it is probably a silicate. But when you look, it's got some tiny inclusions. If you look long enough it feels as if you're staring into it, not at it; into. But that's me. I would, wouldn't I?'

'Mm. Perhaps. Then perhaps not.'

Meg laid the flat side in her palm and weighed it.

'This way, it's a heart,' she said. 'But if you turn it this way, the profile is more like that of a car.'

'A car. It is. It is,' said Colin. 'One of those tinted-windowed things they drive round here.'

'Ah, drivers,' said Meg. '"The bimbos of Lower Slobovia," as I've heard tell. I know what you mean. They don't take kindly to being carved up by my bike; not one bit they don't.'

'I've been in a ditch many a time on their account,' said Colin. 'What are they hiding that's so important?'

'Cotton-woolled kids, mainly. But I do agree.'

'Wait a minute,' said Colin. He took the stone from Meg's hand. 'There's something else. Wait a minute.'

He held the stone sideways on. 'No.' He put the stone down on the cushion and sat back, his hands behind him.

'What's the matter?' said Meg.

'No. No. No. No. No. No. No. No. No.'

'Oh, cripes,' said Meg. 'Colin, I thought you said this was social. Come on. Oi. Off. Shift your bum. Move. Over there. Now.'

Colin went wide round the table and sat in the chair, watching the stone.

'What is it?' said Meg.

'Crow. Upper mandible. Crow. Carrion crow. *Corvus corone corone*. You know. Corneille noire; cornacchia nera; frân dyddyn; varona chernaya; wroniec; nokivaris; Rabenkrähe; svart kråka . . .'

'Right,' said Meg. 'And not before time. Colin, what is it about crows with you? Eric put in his notes that when he suggested you came here you asked whether I was a witch. Now that's something I get, in one form or another, nearly every time, especially from goofed-up males and loud-mouthed honking know-alls. I'm used to it. But then you asked if I liked crows. It was the first thing you asked me. Did I like crows? So what is it?'

'No.'

'Sorry, but Yes. The stone's trying to help you. Listen to it. What's it telling you? What is it you see?'

'No.'

'Colin. You're not your ordinary anorak routine twitcher with binoculars round your neck and a notebook in your hand. And you don't collect train numbers on Crewe station. You've published; and published damned well, from what I've read about you. So why do you get spooked when it comes to crows?'

'Co-authored,' said Colin. 'Mainly the raptors, especially

kestrel, *Falco tinnunculus*, commonly windhover. Its usual prey is the smaller mammals, such as mice and voles; even young rabbits. I did not write the chapter on the *Corvidae*.'

'Why not?'

'Meg. Please.'

'Go there. Tell me. Now's your chance. The stone's on your side.'

'Please. I can't.'

'You can. Come on, chuckles. What's up with crows?'

'And witches. I can't tell them apart. Fact from metaphor. They're every part alike the same to me.'

'Really? I did wonder what all that was about.'

'What all what was about?'

'I was wondering whether you'd say without being shoved.'

'Say what?'

'Eric said that before you went in to see him you'd caused quite a stramash in the waiting area when you shouted at a small kid and his granny.'

'Oh, that.'

'Oh, yes, that. What got into you?'

'She was reading a story to him,' said Colin. 'About a boy going to a witch's house. And I had a flashback. I couldn't help it.'

'Was it a flashback of something that happened or of a dream?'

'I don't know.'

'Can't you remember? Can't you tell the difference?'

'Usually I can. But this was so clear. So vivid. It felt that it had happened. Happened to me. Once.'

'Is it a retrieved flashback from before you were thirteen?'

'It must be.'

'Can you see it now?'

'I don't want to.'

'Tell me.'

'Do I have to?'

'It matters, Colin. It matters a lot. I don't mock witches.'

'I'm in a room in a big house. I don't remember how I've come to be here. Crows are perched on the windowsills outside. And there's a witch, she's standing over me. I know she's a witch. She's all in black, with a cord round her waist. I'm lying on the floor. I can't move.'

'Does she look like me?' said Meg.

'—No. She's older. Fatter and older.'

'You hesitated.'

'Only because you asked. Though sometimes you do have that look about you. When you scare me.'

'Go on,' said Meg.

'She has a wide mouth, thin lips, and her head is sitting on her shoulders as if she hasn't got a neck, and her eyes are close together. Her legs are thin, too. She looks like a crow: a big fat crow. And she goes out of the room and locks the door. I'm alone, and the crows are watching me. But I know she'll be back. She's said she'll eat me. And I've wet myself. And it's all going to happen again to the boy at the doctor's. I've got to save him. I've got to stop the story.'

'Is that why the flashback's so clear?'

'I've had it before. All my life since the flashbacks began. It's the worst of them. Sometimes I dream it and wake and it's still there and I have to go on watching it.'

'How does it end?'

'It just ends. Until the next time, when it starts all over again. But the crows are real. They peck on the windows and the door of the Bergli in the night. I hear them, though I don't see them.'

'At night?' said Meg. 'You'll tell me if I'm wrong, but crows aren't nocturnal.'

'They're not,' said Colin. 'But these are. They must be. That's why I'm terrified of crows. It's selective ornithophobia. I love birds; but these are different. They're witches. They know.'

'There's more, isn't there?' said Meg. 'Come on. Now. It's

now, Colin. I don't want to have to crank you up to this pitch again.'

Colin stared at the profile of the stone. He shook. Meg was still.

'Help me.'

Meg was still.

'Help me.'

'The stone, Colin. The stone.'

'Yes. All right. No.'

'The stone.'

'Yes.'

He clenched his fists on either side of his face and shut his eyes.

'I'm at school. Walking. By myself. On a path. Through the fields. By a wood.'

'How old are you?'

'Thirteen years ten months and six days.'

'Go on.'

'There's something fluttering. In the grass. I go to look. It's a crow. A carrion crow. *Corvus corone corone.* Caught in a mess of barbed wire. I don't know what to do. I can't leave it. I'll have to touch it. I've got to touch it. I've got to touch the witch. Pick it up. I reach down. Its feathers and scales. I try to free it. It pecks me. Makes me bleed. I try again. It's tangled in the wire. I get it free. It's broken a leg and a wing. I don't know what to do. There's no one else. Just me. It's in pain. I can't save it. I have to kill it. I must. It's the only thing. But I don't know how. Wring its neck. That's quickest. Kindest. I don't want to hurt it. I don't want it to suffer. I want to help. It's still a bird. I must help; even when it's a witch. It's still a bird. I must help the bird. I try. But I can't. I can't do it properly. I don't know how. It croaks. It cries. I can't do it. I'm not strong enough. And I'm bleeding. Red. Blood. I hold it by the throat with both hands. I hold it out. In front of me. I squeeze. I've got to choke it. Strangle it. It flaps its wing and claws my wrists with its leg. It's looking at me. Its eye. It's looking. I'm squeezing. As hard as I can. My arms hurt. I can't feel my hands. It flaps its wing. It's clawing. I don't let go. I can't. I'm crying. Its eyelid half closes. And opens. I mustn't let go. Not now. The lid closes. Opens. Half closes. Opens. It's looking at me. Closes. The claws stop. The wing flaps. I hold. Tight. Tight as I can. The body's jerking. I walk back to school. Holding. The crow's still. I've killed the bird. Have I killed the witch? Have I? Have I? Teachers see me. They're shouting. They throw the bird away. Won't let me bury it. I'm—' He opened his eyes.

'OK, Colin. Rest, love.'

'No! That's the start. Only the start. Ever since. They've known. The crows have known. They know what I did. They know it was me. They know. They wait.'

'Shut your eyes again,' said Meg. 'Is the crow still hurting?'

'Yes.'

'What do you want to do?'

'I want to stop it.'

'Stop what?'

'Stop the hurt.'

'How are you going to do that?'

'I don't know.'

'You're a big boy now. Squeeze harder.'

'I can't.'

'Try.'

'How?'

'First of all,' said Meg, 'you must stop blaming yourself. The crows do not know. They really do not. You only think they do. They are not waiting. They do not come to you at night. You want them to. So that you can go on hurting as well.'

'Meg. Please. No. Please.'

'Look again, Colin. You're holding the crow. What's the worst part?'

'I can't look.'

'You can. Look. What's the worst? The very worst.'

'It's flapping. It's dead. But it's flapping. The feathers are alive. The bird isn't.'

'Worse than that.'

'Its eye.'

'Worse than that.'

'The lid. Half closing and opening.'

'Worse than that.'

'Nothing.'

'Look closer.'

'No. I can't.'

'Look closer, Colin.'

'Meg.'

'Closer, Colin. Closer.'

'What's happening?'

'Look. Go to where it hurts most and say what it says to you.'

'—Black.'

'Yes?'

'Black. Shining. Eye.'

'Tell me again.'

'Black. Shining. Eye.'

'Tell me again.'

'Black. Shining—No. Shining. Shining. Ink! Black ink!'

'Go to the ink and say what it says to you.'

'Ink.'

'Tell me again.'

'Ink. Black ink. Shining. Ink.'

'Tell me again.'

'Black. Shining. Ink—No! Not ink! Water! Black shining water! A river! I can't swim! I'll drown! A cave! No! Shining! Shining sky! Stars! No! Galaxies! I see galaxies! Galaxies! More! More than—More! I see! I see! Wonders!'

Colin opened his eyes. 'Meg! Oh, Meg!'

'Where is the crow now?'

'It's gone. It's not there. It's not there.'

'And the other crows?'

'Not any. Gone. All gone. All.'

'Not gone,' said Meg. 'Free. Not hurting. That crow is not hurting. It knows, Colin. It knows you were trying to help. And you? What do you want to do now?'

'Get back to my work. There's so much to be done. So much.' Colin began to cry. 'So much. The wonders.'

'And that's how you start to squeeze,' said Meg, and reached round his back to give him the box of tissues. 'But it's only the start. You've healed the crow. Now you can pass on.'

'I don't understand,' said Colin.

'You've begun; but that's all. You have to end. Else you can forget your wonders.'

'I don't understand.'

'The Grail Question. That's for you to ask; and to find the answer; not me.'

'"Only the start." You're kind. But please not yet. I have to think about it.'

'Kind? Me kind? You dimmock. You dithering dimmock. You're all the same. Every one of you. Each time. It's there before you, in clear. But you won't see. You say you want help, but as soon as the pain really bites you try to sling in the towel. You'll "have to think about it". I can live with that. But don't think you can call the shots. And don't you ever, ever doorstep me again, pal; not even with stone axes. I'm not here to be switched on at a whim.'

'I'm sorry.'

'This time, "sorry" is needed,' said Meg. There was a knock. 'Come in, Bert. We're through.'

Bert put his head round the door. 'Let's be having you. I've stuck your bike in the boot.'

Colin sat and did not speak. Bert was silent. They came to

the turn to the wood. Bert stopped on the road. 'You'll do at this,' he said. 'I'll not can go with you no further.'

'Yes,' said Colin. He lifted his bicycle from the back of the taxi. 'Thanks.'

'Eh. Youth.'

'Yes?'

'Thee think on, and then.'

Bert drove away.

He slept, and turned, calling to the beasts in Ludcruck. They answered him, the beasts and the cranes, and he was not afraid to hear their singing.

Colin heard the sound of an engine in the quarry and looked out of the window. It was Meg in her black leathers. She stopped at the hut, took off her helmet and gauntlets and shook her hair.

Colin opened the door.

'Hi, Colin. How are you doing?'

'Better,' he said. 'Better, I think. Why are you here, Meg?'

'I want a word with you. On your own midden.'

'You're angry over yesterday,' said Colin.

'Who? Me? I'm never angry. I tell it how it is; that's all I can.'

'And I did something to vex Bert. I don't know what it was.'

'Bert's not vexed,' said Meg.

'He was very short with me.'

'He was not.'

'You don't know what he said.'

'We're both in there rooting for you, Colin, you twerp. And now you're on a roll at last you've got to see it through. Now. Not tomorrow. Not when you've "had a think". Now. You must go for it. And stuff the crows.'

'But you could have phoned.'

'I was afraid you'd do a runner. Can I come in?'

'Please,' said Colin. 'But what's it about?'

Meg pulled the bike up on its rest and lifted a file from a pannier. They went inside.

'Do sit down,' said Colin. 'May I have your jacket? It's warm in here.'

'No thanks. We're not stopping.' Meg put the file on the table and took out a clipboard. She did not sit.

'I want to check on a few things first,' she said. 'It's about your brain scan. When I asked you whether you'd ever been struck by lightning you overreacted. You said, and I quote, "I'm sorry. I didn't mean it. I didn't mean it. Promise I didn't. How can you tell? You weren't there. Why don't you go away? Leave me alone." So I did. And I have done. But, now you've had time to let it soak in, is there anything you want to say about that?'

'No.'

'Nothing at all? Think.'

'I can't.' He wiped his palms on a handkerchief. 'I don't want to.'

'Why are your hands sweating?'

'I don't know. I'm scared.'

'Mm,' said Meg. 'Now then. The other day I called up your earliest medical records. I should have done that first off; obviously. As should the others. Fool that I was and am. You could sue me for negligence, and win.'

'But I wouldn't do that. I wouldn't do that, Meg.'

'You're too generous.'

'But I wouldn't.'

'And ingenuous.'

'I wouldn't, Meg.'

'Anyway, clear as clear, in black and white, there you are, aged twelve, being treated for cardiopulmonary arrest, which had more or less righted itself by the time you reached hospital, though your pulse rate was low and your extremities were mottled. These also resolved over several hours. There's a query marginal note: lightning. Oh, Meg Massey. You ought to be struck off. How dim and stupid can you be not to come up with that from the start? Does it help you?'

'No.'

'I think you're playing silly sods again, Colin. Anyhow, that's when I had a rush of brains to the head. I went to the library and trawled through the local papers after that date. Have a look at this.'

She handed him a copied sheet. Colin took it, and read.

LOCAL BOY'S MIRACLE ESCAPE
Youth Cheats Death on Edge Thanks to Walkers
Double Tragedy Narrowly Averted

He glanced at a photograph of rocks and handed the sheet back. 'No. You read it.'

'As you like,' said Meg. '"On Wednesday last week, twelve-year-old Colin Whisterfield, of Highmost Redmanhey Farm, Hocker Lane, Over Alderley, had a miraculous escape when he was hit by lightning in a freak thunderstorm near Stormy Point. He was found unconscious by two walkers on a ledge by the Iron Gates rocks on Saddlebole. They summoned help, and young Colin was stretchered to a waiting ambulance on Stormy Point and rushed to Macclesfield Hospital, where after three days of observation and tests he was declared fit to go home. One of the walkers, who does not wish to be named, said that he and a companion were on Stormy Point, admiring the views, when they saw a small black cloud form over Saddlebole. Before they could take shelter from what they thought would be a storm, there was a sudden flash of lightning, accompanied by a clap of thunder, and the cloud vanished. They proceeded to Saddlebole to look and were shocked to find young Colin lying on the ledge in front of the rocks. He and the rocks were wet, but astonishingly the trees and the path around were bone dry.

'I've never seen anything like it in all my life,' said the other walker, who also does not wish to be named. 'I thought the lad was gone. He was such a dreadful colour.'

'"The prompt action by the medics almost certainly narrowly averted a double tragedy for Hocker Lane. During the night of 21st November last year, as reported in these pages, Colin's twin sister"—and they do mention her name—"disappeared from Highmost Redmanhey Farm together with a horse that had been tethered in the stable. The horse was discovered safe next morning on an island on Redesmere, but despite frantic efforts by the police, using sniffer dogs, and an inch by inch search of the mere by frogmen, with local volunteers combing the surrounding rhododendron woods, no trace of the young girl was ever found. On both occasions Mr and Mrs Gowther Mossock, the boy's guardians, who farm Highmost Redmanhey, were too upset to comment about the events."'

Colin turned his head aside.

'I wonder why witnesses never want to be identified,' said Meg. 'I bet these two were having it off in the bracken.'

Colin looked back at the photograph of the rocks. He was trembling.

'So it did happen, Colin. And it was you. And it could explain the anomaly in the brain scan. Has that helped?'

'Not really.'

'Well, it's helped me. It makes the episodic memory and isolated retrograde amnesia credible. The hypothetical hyper-thymesia's still the Joker in the pack, but there are other sporadic anomalous claims in the literature concerning the after-effects of lightning strike in humans. One man said it brought on satyriasis, which didn't please his wife; another blamed it for priapism; but I don't think we need go there. A woman in Illinois said she had become psychic after being struck in bed, and that her powers were used by police agencies in locating missing persons. You takes your pick. But one published report caught my eye: a case of alleged significant increase in intelligence on psychological testing after prolonged cardiac arrest in a paediatric patient. If there's anything in that, it could explain a lot. What do you think?'

'I don't know,' said Colin.

'So why are you still sweating?' said Meg.

'I don't know.'

'I'd like to go and have a look at Saddlebole,' said Meg. 'Will you take me there?'

'Now?'

'Yes, please.'

'No,' said Colin. 'I'd rather not.'

'I did say please.'

'Why? Why do you want to go?'

'A hunch. Mainly you. When we went for that walk the night I came here you obviously shied away from showing me when I asked what it was.'

'I didn't want to overcook the lamb.'

'That was quick thinking on your part. Your eyes swerved every which way.'

'I'd rather not.'

'Tough titty. I rather would.'

'I've things to do. Some other time, perhaps.'

'Do them later. I don't want to waste my petrol.'

'All right. All right. But you could have phoned. I must wear my robes.'

'Suit yourself. I'll wait outside while you change.'

'No. The top covering will be enough.'

'Need any help?'

'No. No, thanks.'

Colin opened the box and eased the shirt and bow tie from their tissues. He fitted the gold cufflinks and held the sleeves as he slid his arms into the black gown. Then he brushed the scarlet and blue silk chimere, fitted it over the gown and fastened it with the two buttons. To finish, he slipped the hood of green silk over his shoulders and set the bonnet on his head and adjusted the tassel. He checked in the mirror, and arranged his hair and beard.

'Right,' said Colin.

'You definitely look the business,' said Meg.

Colin locked the hut and they made their way from the quarry to the track. He lifted his gown and chimere to avoid snagging.

'Do you mind if we stay on the track?' said Colin. 'It's safer.'

'How "safer"?' said Meg.

'It's a bit less direct, but it's wider and won't catch on the silk.'

They walked with the wood to their left and the hills to their right.

'You really have got it all, here, haven't you?' said Meg.

'Yes, the landscape is varied.'

'"Varied"? It's spectacular.'

'I suppose it is.'

'What's that over there?'

'Shuttlingslow.'

'It's a stunning shape; iconic.'

'You mean conical.'

'What are you blathering at?' said Meg.

'There's nothing iconic about Shuttlingslow. It is not an icon.'

'Oh dear. Here we go. We're off. What have I done wrong now?'

'An icon,' said Colin, 'is a pictorial representation of a facility available on a computer system that enables the facility to be activated by means of a screen cursor rather than by a textual instruction. Its original, religious, meaning is the figure of Christ, the Virgin Mary or a saint, especially one painted in oil and gilded on a wooden panel and venerated in the Eastern Church.'

'I stand corrected, O Master of Theology,' said Meg.

'Shuttlingslow isn't remotely like an icon. Its form is the result of differential weathering of the Chatsworth and Roaches Carboniferous grits.'

'Do you list swallowing dictionaries under "Recreations"?'

'No.'

'That would be lexicophagy, I suppose,' said Meg.

'Would it?'

'Joke. That is a joke, Colin. Joke. Hah. Hah. Hah. Laugh. You can, if you try.'

'I need to be accurate. I won't put up with sloppiness and imprecision.'

'I'll tell you one thing,' said Meg. 'You certainly do not want to take me to Saddlebole. You do not.'

'When I hear a student object that "Near enough is good enough,"' said Colin, 'I know I'm teaching a fool.'

'Oh, you're in a right bate.'

They walked on.

'That tower spoils the skyline,' said Meg. 'Why's it up there?'

'Sutton Common,' said Colin, not looking. 'Radio relay. It's impressive.'

'It's intrusive.'

'No more than the telescope.'

'I disagree. The telescope is both art and science. That tower is function only.'

'Isn't pure art pure function?' said Colin. 'Like the axe? The axe is the first step to the telescope.'

'I need time out on that one,' said Meg.

'And think of Ethel.'

'Why?'

'The signals from Ethel were "nearly" here before the axe was made.'

'Oh, I like it,' said Meg. 'That's poetry. Not half it isn't.'

They came to a T-junction. On one side was a squat block of

130

conglomerate sandstone in a grassy bank, a clunched mass of pebbles glancing the afternoon.

'What's this?' said Meg.

'The Goldenstone.'

'But it's grey. And packed with quartz. What's it doing here?'

'It's a merestone.'

'A mere stone? I think it's impressive. It's huge.'

'A boundary stone. About twelve tonnes. Come on. Boundaries aren't safe.'

'Why aren't they?'

'Because they're not. They occupy neither space nor time. Boundaries can change apparent realities. They let things through. Come on. If we keep stopping we'll never get to where you want to see before it's too late. In the day, I mean.'

'Right. Shut up, Meg.'

The broad way took them to Stormy Point. Across the waste a hollow path led back into the trees. As they entered, Meg picked up loose pebbles that lay on the ground.

'They're pretty. Hey, this here is a bit of all right.'

They were at a ridge, and the ground dropped to the plain. It was a beech wood, and the trunks were twisted green flames above brown fallen leaves that let nothing grow. The sunlight was shafts between. The path dipped to a saddle and rose beyond.

'It's a cathedral,' said Meg.

'There are your rocks,' said Colin. 'Help yourself.' He kept back.

The rocks stood over the path. One was much taller than the others, a tapering wedge of sandstone. There was a shelf in front. Meg stepped onto it. She patted the stone. 'This is one brute of a bloke, and that's for sure. Come up.'

'I'm happy where I am.'

Meg continued to examine the rock. 'More pebbles,' she said. 'White quartz. Just like the Goldenstone.'

131

'Yes. It's possible it was fetched from near here.'

'Wow. Some job.'

'Quite simple, actually,' said Colin. 'Have you seen all that you want to see?'

'Wait your sweat,' said Meg. She took two of the pebbles that she had gathered on Stormy Point out of her pocket, and with one in each hand began to rub the quartz on the rock.

'Don't do that,' said Colin. 'Don't do it.'

'I'm trying to make that light,' said Meg.

'It's not dark enough,' said Colin. 'Stop.'

'But I like the sound.'

Colin jumped onto the shelf, his robes swelling.

'Stop! I said stop!' He grabbed Meg's wrists.

'Colin. Let go. Let go of me, please.' Her voice was calm.

'You mustn't! Stop it! Stop!'

'I said let go.'

Colin pulled her hands away from the sandstone. Meg moved her forearms in a twist against the joints of his thumbs, and Colin fell on the rock, covered by his robes. The bonnet rolled down the hill.

He pushed himself up. 'Ground strike! Side splash! Assume the position!' He crouched, curled, his head at his knees, covered by his crossed arms, balancing himself on the balls of his feet. 'Don't touch the ground with the hands!'

'You've got the drill OK, but aren't you shutting the stable door a bit late, chum?' said Meg. 'That nag bolted long ago.'

Colin whimpered.

'Didn't it?'

Colin put his hand to his collar and dragged it down. There was a line of thickened discoloured skin on his neck.

'Here. Look.'

'Good job it was raining when you were hit, Colin,' said Meg. 'The flashover may have saved your life.'

Colin moaned. 'This is the mark of the blame I bear in my

neck. This is the sign of loss, of coveting and cowardice that caught me.' He pulled at the hood of green silk. 'This is the token of untruth that I've been snared in, and there's no getting out of it for me for the rest of my life.'

'Oh, give over,' said Meg. 'You piss more than you drink. Come on. Up with you.'

She helped him to stand and get down from the shelf, and she sat with him on a bank of earth by the path.

'No wonder you don't come here, if that's what it does to you. You really are a proper drama queen, aren't you? I've said that to you before.'

'You don't know.'

'I can't if you don't let me in. This isn't the first time, Colin. What happened that day? Tell Aunty Meg.'

He cuddled up to her. 'I never come here. Never since. I didn't mean it.'

'I think you did,' said Meg. 'But mean what?'

'I didn't mean to do it.'

'Do what?'

'Nothing.'

'Have you got that stone in your pocket?'

'Yes. Always, now. How do I get into the mind of who made this?'

'Squeeze,' said Meg. 'Squeeze it. Shut your eyes. Squeeze hard.'

'Why?'

'Don't ask. Do.'

He put his hand into his pocket, and shut his eyes. Lights came in the dark from his lids. Lights from within the stone.

'Squeeze.'

'Flashback! Flashback!'

'Now, Colin. While it's there. Now. It's your chance. You may not have another. You're safe. I'm holding you. Go for it.'

'I can't. I did so much wrong.'

'You can. You've got to learn to forgive yourself. Whatever

133

it is. No one else is blaming you. No one else cares. And you know I can't be doing with whining self-pity. Set it free.'

'Set it free?'

'Set it free.'

'Like the crow?'

'Set it free.'

He looked at the pebbles in the rock, and shut his eyes again.

'Silicon,' said Meg. 'Moonlight. You have the black stone. Black blacker than black. The Grail. The Question. "What is this thing? What does it mean? Whom does it serve?" Ask. Squeeze. Squeeze hard. Squeeze harder. As if carbon. Squeeze carbon. Squeeze carbon as far as it will. As far as carbon can.'

'But if it's not carbon . . .'

'Faith.'

'How?'

'Belief, Colin.'

'I can't.'

'Reality. You can.'

'No.'

'Truth.'

'Yes.'

'What do you get?'

'Yes. Yes.'

'What do you get?'

'I get. I get. Get—diamond!'

'At last. At final, bleeding last. Colin, you've done it.'

'Diamond. Eternal.'

He lay against her. The Edge trembled with sobbing.

'They say. They say.'

'Yes.'

'They say.'

'Who say?'

'They say. They say. They say there are. Men. In the hill. Horses. A king. In the hill. Here. Asleep. Waiting. Waiting.'

'For what?'

'Waiting. Until it's Time.'

'I understand.'

'They mustn't wake. Ever. Not till it's Time.'

'I understand you, Colin.'

'But it is Time. It's Time now. I need. I need them now. I must wake them. They'll find her. They will.'

'Oh, you poor lad.'

'So I come. I come here. I hit the rock. The pebbles. I'm calling. "Wake up! It's Time! Find her! It's Time!" Then the lights. The lightning: blue, silver, blue silver. Lightning. All around. Thunder. "Wake up! You must find her!" Then. There's a cloud above. Not big. Right over me. It's starting to rain. Heavy. There's the man. The tall man. Thin. He's old. He's very old. He should be dead. But he's not. He can't. He's angry. He's looking at me. His eyes. He curses me. His eyes! He curses me with forgetting and remembering, dreaming and waking! No! Flashback! Dreams! Always dreams! Always him! He puts his fate on me! To guard! To dream! For all Time!'

'Wha-hey, you're in lumber now sure enough, Colin, my love. You're down in the collective now. Well down. You're on Tom Tiddler's ground, and there's no picking up gold and silver for you here. There is not. And do you wonder? They're the Sleepers. You don't mess with those guys. You don't mix it with them, my friend. Once they wake, it's curtains.'

'But are they real?'

'Does it make any difference?' said Meg. 'With your mind, and your work and what you've said, the question shouldn't worry you. "What were the fairy tales, they will come true."'

'You're not laughing at me,' said Colin.

'I never laugh at. That's not my job. And what's the point? But don't be too clever, Colin. You must not let yourself be prisoner to deep place; to the Edge. Or Ludchurch.' She stood and gave him a hand up. 'And hold fast on that stone. You've not done yet. At least we know now why you smashed the glass. Don't forget your hat.'

I have a Story, he said.

Tell me, said the other.

When Crane set the Stone Spirit to send eagles to feed the stars and went back to fly for ever between Earth and Sky the world grew full of life; and the Stone Spirit made the Hunter to walk beneath to watch the herds, and the Bull to go before him to show the way. Then the Stone Spirit reached to the Hill of Death and Life and took red earth and shaped it to be people and opened their mouths so that they might eat, and gave them legs and hands so that they might hunt. And it parted the people, each to hold the other, so that they would grow more. Then it gave to the people spirits of the beasts, so that they would keep those spirits safe; and those beasts they did not eat. Nor could the people hold people that were of their spirit, for that would wrong the world.

What is your spirit? said the other.

I am of Crow and of Crane, and I call to Wolf.

What is your song?

To dance in Ludcruck to cut the rock and to keep the sun from death.

That is a true Story, said the other.

'—"to light you to bed."—' Colin lifted the axe from the corner, wiped the edge of the blade with a rag, picked up an empty basket and went out to the log stack. '—"And here comes a chopper to chop off your head."' By the stack there was a treadle grindstone. He set one foot on the plate and pressed down, letting the plate lift at the end of the turn. When the stone was at the right speed Colin held the blade against it to lie with the spin, moving the steel to firm the shoulder. The noise clattered in the rocks, rang on the quarry side. Then he

136

moved the blade to balance the shoulder, tested the blade with his thumb, and took a whetstone from his pocket and fined the edge. He looked along the line to check the curve.

He pulled logs out from the stack, ash, holly, thorn, and put them next to a block of elm, criss-crossed by hatchings of old cuts. He placed a log on end with care to firm it on the block, braced his legs apart, breathed in, and out, and in, loosened his shoulders, gripped the helve, and swung.

'Chip.'

The log split into equal parts, each falling aside. He picked one and stood it upright, and swung.

'Chop.'

He set the other, and swung.

'Chip.'

He gathered the four pieces, dropped them into the basket and put another log on the elm.

'Chip. Chop. Chip.'

He held and swung the axe so that it fell in an arc and its own weight did the work.

'Chip. Chop. Chip. Chip. Chop. Chip. Chip. Chop. Chip. Last. Man's. Dead.'

He went on until the basket was full. He took the axe back to the hut and brought in the basket and settled it by the hearth. He wiped the axe head and the helve and dribbled fine oil along the blade and smoothed it over with his fingers. Then he placed the axe back in its corner and cleaned his hands.

Colin lifted a toolbox from a shelf and left the hut. He went to the dishes, and stood before one of the focus rings. He looked at it for a long time, and smiled. 'Hah. Yes. OK. Right. Now then.' He opened the toolbox and picked two spanners, fitted them against a nut and bolt at the base and put pressure on to slacken the thread. 'That's the way to do it.'

'Hang about, Colin. Half a sec.'

Colin let go of the spanners and jolted back.

'You?'

''Fraid so, my love. You're coming good, son. But not yet. You can't disconnect yet. It's not Time yet; for you.'

'What? Meg? Is it? Meg?'

'I couldn't tell you until you made your mind up. But you're acting a bit previous. You're not there yet.'

'Meg. What do you mean? What's happening?'

'You don't need me now. You had to find it for yourself. I'm only a mirror. Think of the moon, Colin. That's my job. It's what I am. It's all I can be.'

'No. I do need you. I need you a lot.'

'Not any more. It's over and out now, my darling. The last bit's all yours. I can't go there.'

'Meg. No.'

'Colin. Yes. You're OK. You've done us proud. And Colin, you just think on. Think on. If the Sleeper wakes, the Dream dies.'

'Meg. Meg. Meg. You don't say goodbye. You said.'

Silence.

Colin ran to the hut. He jabbed the telephone.

'The number you have dialled has not been recognised. Please check and try again.'

He jabbed.

'The number you have dialled has not been recognised. Please check and try again.'

Again.

'The number you have dialled has not been recognised. Please check and try again.'

'Shut up, you stupid cow!'

Colin laid the telephone down until he had control of his breathing. He picked it up and pressed each number firmly, and paused, with care.

'The number you have dialled has not been recognised. Please check and try again.'

'Damn you!'

Colin looked at the telephone file. He put in Bert's number.

'The number you have dialled has not been recognised. Please check and try again.'

He scrabbled among the papers on his dresser, but could not find Bert's card.

'Hello. Hello. Oh, come on! Hello.'

'Directory Enquiries. Kay speaking, Professor Whisterfield. There is a charge for this call. How can I help you?'

'Please. I want the number of High Forest Taxis, Macclesfield. Please. Hurry.'

'Bear with me one moment, sir.'

'Hurry. It's important.'

'Bear with me, sir.'

'Of course. I'm sorry.'

Colin scrabbled on the dresser again.

'Hello, sir.'

'Yes. Yes.'

'I'm afraid no such firm is listed.'

'It is! It must be! I've used it! Often! All the time!'

'It may have gone out of business. I'm sorry, sir. I'm afraid I can't help you.'

He threw the telephone from him.

'Hello, sir? Hello?'

Colin ran his bicycle through the quarry and mounted at the track. He did not have his helmet. He bounced over the ruts and stones and potholes and cobbles, pedalling hard, onto the road and along past Beacon Lodge and the Castle Rock lay-by to the drop at Armstrong Farm, crouched over his handlebars, to the bend at Whinsbrow by the notice THIS HILL IS STILL DANGEROUS straight down from Rockside to the roundabout at London Road. He braked and trailed his foot to veer to the right, among the flocks of cars. He stood on the pedals. Tyres squealed. He went over the station bridge and into Brook Lane, to Row-of-Trees, by Lindow Moss, along Seven Sisters Lane to Toft.

He turned onto the drive without looking. The gates were closed. He skidded and hit the woodwork sideways, but did not fall. He dropped the bicycle to open the gate. It was chained, and an unclasped padlock joined the links. Then he saw the board. Meller Braggins Established 1836. FOR SALE OR TO LET. And the estate agent's address and telephone number.

Colin opened the gate and wheeled his bicycle through. He walked down the drive. Weeds had taken over the gravel. The bushes were unkempt and the rhododendrons were invading the front door, reaching into the porch. The windows were shuttered.

He left his bicycle and went around the house. He walked clockwise. The lawns were seeding grass. The flowerbeds had flowers that he remembered, but they were losing against invading growth. He came to the French windows of the library. They too were shuttered. He looked out at Beeston bluff.

He went on, and came to the greenhouse and the stable block. He stopped. There was a white van in the yard. Someone was whistling. Colin knew the tune. The wind, the wind, the wind blows high—

There was a man on a ladder, painting the transoms and mullions of a window.

'Excuse me,' said Colin.

The man wiped his brush and laid it across the paint can hanging from a rung.

'Eh up, squire. Are you all right? What can we do for you?'

'I don't want to disturb you,' said Colin.

'You're not,' said the man.

'What's happening here?'

'Not a lot.'

'What are you doing?'

'Oh, just giving the old place a lick and a promise.'

'Who lives here?'

'Nobody.'

'No one?'

'Not while I've been looking after it.'

'How long is that?'

'Must be a three year, give or take. I do the odd bit of bodging so it doesn't get any worse than it is. But, between you and me, it's nobbut a hindrance. Too big for living, too small for business or flats. And the gardens are in shit order. They're neither use nor ornament.'

'Who was here last?'

'You'd best ask the office. What's up wi' thee? What's mithering you?'

'I know this place,' said Colin. 'I was here a few days ago. And someone else was here. They were. They were here too.'

'Well, they're not now, anyroad,' said the man. 'You want to take more water with it.'

'Would it be possible for me to see inside?' said Colin. 'I don't wish to waste your time. It would take only a moment. Just the hall and the library will be enough.'

'I'm the governor of this gang,' said the man, 'and we're not on piece work. Help yourself. It's all fetching night.' He came down from the ladder, took a bunch of keys from his overalls and unlocked the back door. Colin went with him into the closed house. They passed through the kitchen.

'I know this,' said Colin. 'It's the hall.'

'You're not wrong,' said the man. 'Here.' He switched on a maintenance light.

'And this door's to the library,' said Colin. 'It is. It has to be.'

'Correct.' The man opened the door and pressed another switch.

The curtains were drawn across the shutters. He knew them. The furniture was draped with dustsheets, but he could see the shapes: the chaise longue and the deep chair on either side of

141

the fireplace; the low table, the drinks cabinet, the clock. The chandeliers hung in cotton covers. The walls were lined with empty shelves; they had no books.

'You OK, mate?'

'Yes. Yes. Thank you. Thank you. I've seen what I have to,' said Colin.

'You're looking badly,' said the man. 'Let's get you outside and sit you down.'

'Thanks. Thanks,' said Colin.

Colin sat on a step. The lines of the world returned.

'You seem to know your way around,' said the man. 'I'll give you that.'

'Yes. Parts. But it doesn't matter. I've taken up enough of your time.'

'I'll be right,' said the man. 'So long as me brush doesn't dry. That's what they say.'

'Thank you. Thank you again.'

'Cheers.'

'I'm so sorry,' said Colin. 'I didn't introduce myself. Whisterfield. Colin Whisterfield.' He held out his hand. The man wiped his on his overalls. 'Pleased to meet you, Colin,' he said. 'Call me Bert.'

Colin rode back along the drive to the gate, opened and closed it, replaced the lock. He rode blind by Seven Sisters Lane, Lindow Moss, Row-of-Trees, Brook Lane, London Road and up the Front Hill.

At Castle Rock lay-by he left his bicycle and ran along the path to the Rock. Its smooth quarried surface drew him to the point, and the point drew him beyond. He ran across the last ledge. There was nothing but the point and air, calling him. Three strides to an end. Three strides and then no more. His head no more rampicked by the stars. No more agate with dreams. No more. But the world swung. He pitched. His face was over the brink, his arms beside. He saw the grooves carved by rain down the rock, and the fields beneath. He could not move. His body was clamped. He pulled his hands back and gripped. He pushed, keeping every part of him against the rock. His eyes lost the vastitude and were seeing grains and pebbles, back and back, over the ancient river, until his feet met the ledge. But even here he could not stand. He rolled, ignoring pain, until he was further than his own length from the ledge. He turned onto his knees, facing away, and stood. To the south, on the safe land, the telescope was tilted, pointing at him. He clutched the black stone.

I have a Story.

Tell me your Story, said the other.

The world was full, and the people hunted, and the sun was young. Then two people of the Crow held each other, and the Stone Spirit wept and the sun moved its face. Then came cold, and the herds went. The Hunter and the people followed them and the world was empty; but the Bull stayed. And every night of winter he comes above the hills, watching to see that there is life; and the Stone Spirit looks to send out eagles from its head to feed the stars.

And because the Crow flesh brought the cold they stayed to dance and cut and sing in Ludcruck to make new the Bull and the beasts on the wall of the sky cave above the waters for the time when all will be again, with the Hunter striding. But if we do not dance and cut and sing and make the beasts new on the sky wall the Stone Spirit will not send eagles.

And who is it that you hold? said the other.

No one. She and the child went to the ice. No one is left to hold. No child to teach. I am alone. After me, no one will give my flesh to the sky, take my bones to the nooks of the dead. The sun will not come back. The Stone Spirit will not send eagles. The world will end.

That is a true Story, said the other.

*

Colin woke. 'Doctor Knickerbocker, Knickerbocker, number nine. He sure got drunk on a bottle of wine.' He could not tell between memory and dream. There was a child singing in the quarry. He squirmed out of his bunk and opened the door and listened.

'Rosy apple, lemon and a pear.

Bunch of roses she shall wear.'

He went onto the grass, but could see no one.

'Be careful!' he shouted. 'Mind you don't fall! The quarry's dangerous!'

There was laughter.

'Be careful! Where are you?'

He dressed in a hurry and went out again.

'Hello!'

'Gold and silver by her side.

She shall be a bride.'

'Where are you?'

More laughter.

'Don't be silly! You could hurt yourself!'

He went up the path out of the quarry and walked all around the rim, checking. He called once more, but there was no answer. He went back by the main entrance.

'Careful on the rocks! You could slip and sprain your ankle!'

'I'll be careful, Col, don't you worry.'

He was between the dishes.

'You?'

'Of course. Who else?'

'Where are you?'

'Everywhere. Come and find me. Let's play hide-and-seek. You'll be "It".'

'No going out of the quarry,' said Colin.

'Mardy, mardy mustard.

Your head is made of custard.'

'And no going in the hut.'

144

'Ha, ha, ha, hee, hee, hee.

You can't catch me for a penny cup of tea.'

'Ready?'

'Yes. This is fun.'

'One, two, three, four, five, six, seven, eight, nine . . .'

'Ha, ha, ha, hee, hee, hee.

The elephant nests in a rhubarb tree.'

'. . . ninety-one, ninety-two, ninety-three, ninety-four, ninety-five, ninety-six, ninety-seven, ninety-eight, ninety-nine. One hundred. Coming, ready or not. No barleys.'

Colin left the focus and looked around. The quarry was still. Nothing moved. He watched. He listened. Then he went to the entrance, and came back, crossing the ground to and fro. There were no prints in the mud, no moss on the rockery steps had been disturbed, no grass or reeds bent. He moved forward over unmarked dew.

'Take her by the lily-white hand.'

The sound had no direction, but was outside the dishes and his head.

'—lily-white hand.'

He moved along the floor of the quarry.

'Lead her across the water.'

The rhododendrons were the only cover. He thrashed through them. Nothing.

'Lead her across the water.'

There was the hut.

'I said no going in the hut! I said!'

Laughter.

He went clockwise around the outside. Nothing. He ran. Nothing. He ran the other way, widdershins. Nothing. He looked inside. There was nowhere else.

'Lead her across the water.'

He went back to the dishes and to the focus. 'I give up. You win. "Olly, olly all in, no back bargains."'

'Oh, Col. You big sissy. You know where I am. Try harder.'

He went through the quarry again. Nothing. He went back to the dishes. The quarry was still; only a small wind.

There was a giggle, not at the focus. It had to be at the far end. The adit. He went towards the gate, the locked iron gate into the hill.

'Give her a kiss and say goodbye.'

The sound was in the tunnel. He unfastened the gate. He stepped up. 'Relieve-o!'

'Relieve-o!' Was it an echo?

'She is the fairest daughter.' Not an echo.

He moved in as far as the goblin gold, the edge of the dark. He took the stone from his pocket and held it before him.

'Rosy apple, lemon and a pear.

Bunch of roses she shall wear.

Gold and silver by her side.

She shall be a bride.'

Triboluminescence flickered at the far end. He went on.

'Take her by the lily-white hand.

Lead her across the water.'

The small black figure appeared limned in moonlight from the pebbles. He moved slowly.

'Don't be scared,' he said.

They moved towards each other.

'Lead her across the water.'

As she came nearer, she grew.

'Lead her across the water.'

The day behind him, and the pebbles around, lit the tunnel. She was now his size, but black, without feature.

'I'm not scared, Col. Not now. Are you?'

'No.'

He did not pause. He could touch her dark, but he did not. They were face to face, surrounded by light from the quartz.

'Give her a kiss and say goodbye.'

She reached out to him. He reached to her. They clasped. He held the stone against her spine. The stone light quenched the moon.

'She is the fairest daughter.'

'Who are you?' he said.

'You.'

I sang and danced, and cut a woman for me to fetch a child for me to teach to dance and sing and cut. But you have come, not she.

That is a true Story, said the other.

He went to the dish. 'Meg.'

'Yes, Colin.'

'I've been to Toft.'

'Then you'll know.'

'Yes. And I've found her.'

'Where?'

'Here.'

'So you understand. You asked the Question.'

'Yes.'

'Do you understand the answer?'

'Yes.'

'So?'

'I've stopped the hurt.'

'What a long way to market, eh?'

'Yes.'

'But that's the way it is and has to fare, my love. You end at the start. You told me yourself.'

'I did. Yes. I did.'

'We are always with you, Colin. Always have been. Always shall be. All three.'

'Three?'

'Three.'

'Her too?'

'Her too.'

'Her in the room?'

'Her in the room. Trinity. You are nothing without her. She is the shadow that shapes your light. The moon, Colin. Ever strong; ever dying; ever young; the same. We are the Three. With you. Of you. In you. No need to fear or find.'

'If you could have told me, from the start—'

'Ah. "If ifs and ands were pots and pans, there'd be no trade for tinkers." "If" is a big word, Colin. You had to do it yourself. I said so all along. I did tell you.'

'What's that noise?'

'Why don't you look?'

Colin turned his face to the other dish.

'It's only a crow,' he said. 'Carrion crow. *Corvus corone corone*.'

'Only a crow.'

'Yes. They're very common.'

'Then do it.'

'Yes.'

'That's the ticket. That's the ticket for soup.'

'Yes.'

'Now, Colin.'

'Yes.'

'Forgive yourself. Accept.'

'Yes.'

'Now, Colin.'

'Now, Meg.'

'And be.'

The wind was on the struts.

'Knickerty. Knackerty.'

The spanners gripped.

'Now. Now. Now.'

He disarmed the focus.

Colin left his robes and walked by Seven Firs and Goldenstone and Stormy Point to Saddlebole. He stepped up to the shelf and touched the quartz and laid his cheek against the rough of the sand. 'I'm sorry,' he said. 'I am sorry. I was wrong. I was so wrong. It is not Time. Sleep on.' He went around the scarp to Castle Rock. The telescope moved in azimuth and elevation to lock onto him. He held the black stone: the stone that held stars and galaxies, all heavens in the hand that had held its making. He went to the thrust of the rock above the air and looked down. He looked up. He walked along the brink, along the line of nothing, between sky and ancient river. He turned from the rock towards the dish. It waited. He spoke.

'Listen.'

I see a new Story. I see a Dream.

Tell me, said the other.

'I'll tell you. I've got to tell you.'

I sang and danced and cut the woman. I sang and danced and I cut strong. I cut with the last bone of the Mother, to fetch the woman. But you have come.

'I must tell you.'

I am spirit. I am peace. Take the Stone. Take the bone of the Mother.

'I will.'

Sing, dance, cut. Bring back the sun.

'I shall.'

It is a true Story, said the other. It is a true Dream. Sleep now.